Urban Gothic

Stephen Coghlan

ACKNOWLEDGEMENTS

Thank you, Neil Gaiman, whose works inspired me to dream.

Thank you, Kyanite Publishing, for taking a chance on my dreams.

Thank you, Moss Whelan, for kicking my ass to get this done.

Thank you, all of you wounded warriors, who carry your scars.

Thank you, all of you, who served so we can enjoy a life where we can dream.

You are not forgotten

Paperback ISBN: 978-1-7774408-0-0
Ebook ISBN: 978-1-7774408-1-7
Cover design by Sophia LeRoux
Editing by B.K. Bass
Cover image © depositphotos.com
www.darkbrewpress.com

CHAPTER 1

The door closed with finality. As always, the tune played in his head. It was a familiar song; one that had become ingrained from years of singing it with enthusiasm until he had become driven by survival instead of ambition; until his energy was better spent defending his right to enjoy fresh air and unmonitored walks.

Red light, green light, off the floor,
Shuffle up, buckle up, out the door.

Walking stiffly into the madness of the city, Alec LeGuerrier was deaf to the noises about him as the song continued its inexorable drone with every step he took.

If my chute don't open wide,
I got another one by my side.

The air was normally crisp this time of year, but the atmosphere of the night weighed heavily on him. It forced him to push his body to match the cadence of the tune. He had always loved chanting the next line—screaming it, even—in his youth.

And if that chute don't open too,
Watch your ass, I'm coming through!

It wasn't that long ago that he had been young, but the reality of life had worn him down and aged him prematurely. It wasn't the constant concern of bills, career, or family that bothered him. Rather, it was the smell of death permanently entrenched in his nostrils; it was the emptiness inside, the fact there was no one left around him who could understand what he had seen, what he had done, and why he hadn't had a choice. It was the stress of taking his place within society and being what everyone else considered human that bothered him.

In order to fit in with society, Alec had found a job—with the help of his parole officer—and rented an apartment in a low-cost area of a high-cost city. He dressed in plain, non-descript clothes. He tried his best to be nobody.

At work, he was invisible. He spent all day in the crowded hospital, and was ignored while he scrubbed, mopped, and polished the halls to an unnatural sheen. Losing himself in his tasks, he was able to turn off his mind and shut out the horrors of the past that still plagued him. Maybe that was why he had volunteered—no, *begged*—for the night shift?

He loved the daily commute. In the summer, the day's last light was just fading away as he journeyed to work; the night air was less oppressive and offered salvation from the glaring sun, and he returned to a budding dawn and the realisation that a new day had arrived. In winter, the tranquil darkness was sometimes clear enough to see a star or two despite the city lights that reflected off of the snow.

In the night, he felt at peace. In the darkness, he felt a glimmer of hope. In the silence, he felt the vibrancy of life. As he walked home each morning, he shed his worries with the rising sun. Sometimes he thought he might awaken from the nightmare to find his friends still alive. Maybe one sunrise would see him awaken as a young man; able to change his future now that he had been forewarned.

I'll splatter high, I'll splatter wide.
I'll splatter all over the countryside.

With every step, his keys jangled, his wallet swung, and the tiny pill rattled in its bottle. It, too, was a requirement of his humanity—a requirement for his pseudo-freedom. The pills muted his emotions and muddled his mind. He didn't want to take them, but he had been ordered to keep himself subdued, and a refusal brought penalties he did not wish to pay.

Once his shift was done and the sun had risen, he would pop the last pill in his mouth, before meandering into the growing dawn to present his information to the local pharmacy. There, he would receive another collection of those tiny capsules to numb his mind and let him sleep dreamlessly; free from nightmares, free from memories, and free from the guilt of having survived.

Unlike Kiso, who was buried in the earth.

Unlike Frederick, who lay sleeping in a chemical-induced stupor, trapped inside a charred and immobile lump of ruined flesh.

Unlike Sylvain, who had surrendered to his darkest thoughts and washed away his own regrets with alcohol and pills until his heart had failed.

Ducking into an unlit alley, Alec embraced his own darkness until it felt like he was flying, floating far from the ground; unbound, unleashed, and free of all of life's restraints.

You'll find my leg up in a tree,
and then you'll find the rest of me.

And then his feet refused to move. Something he had never seen before in that blind tunnel of brick and mortar broke his trance. Three costumed crazies sashayed about a prostrate body. A woman lay on the ground, her violet eyes wide with fear, blood welling from wounds in her shoulders and legs, hands raised in a feeble attempt to defend herself.

If I die with my hands on my chest
Tell my Ma I did my best.

Every lick of sense Alec had left pleaded with him to keep walking and ignore what he'd seen, and alarm bells rang in his head like the klaxons of some far-away firebase, roaring that this wasn't his problem; it wasn't his duty to become involved. The noise fell silent to his conscience. How would he live with himself if he didn't help this woman?

The voice Alec spoke in was deep and clear; meant to be heard over the chaos of war, over the crack of guns and thunderous explosions.

"Stop."

The single word echoed off the concrete and asphalt; slowly diffusing as it climbed into the empty sky.

If I die with my hands by my side
Tell the sarge I died o' pride.

A twisted, warped, and terrifying clown laughed in response. He had thin blood-red lips, teeth that were chipped and had been filed to jagged points, and small sunken eyes that smoldered like brimstone. As he trembled, so too did the crude mace he wielded. It was little more than a knotted branch, and had been covered in tar and dipped in glass shards and metal fragments. The sinister jester's words came out in the hissing chorus of a thousand broken chimes clashing.

"He can see through the façade."

As his two companions turned to face Alec, he felt an uncanny calmness sweep over him. For the first time in years, he had a purpose, a duty, and a reason to be.

The first foe to advance was tall and lanky with bronzed skin that glowed in the darkness. He wore a long jacket tied about his loins that hid little beneath, and laughed too, but in body only, for no sound emerged from his throat. He carried a blood-covered spear with a wickedly-hooked bill that had been forged into the shape of a raven's beak. When he tapped the weapon against a wall, the steel rang on the brick like an otherworldly gong.

Trying not to take his eyes from him, Alec spied an empty liquor bottle that had either helped someone celebrate or wallow in despair. Grabbing the neck of the vessel with his left hand, he tapped the base against his thigh in time to the rhythm in his head.

If I die o' clutchin' my ass
Tell my dad I died of gas.

Thanks to the narrow alley, the spearman could not swing his weapon from side-to-side, and was forced to aim an overhead strike. Stepping away from the descending blade, Alec let it bite into the ground. Planting his foot upon the haft, he launched himself up and brought his improvised club down on the spearman's skull. The bottle shattered, stunning the tall man, who reflexively stumbled backwards, both hands clutching his head in agony.

Lunging forward, Alec mercilessly drove the jagged remains into his foe's throat, shredding the delicate flesh in a fountain of blood. Gurgling, the spearman collapsed to his knees. Alec smashed his own knee into his opponent's face, flattening him so he could advance past his soon-to-be corpse.

With a roar, the other two assailants charged, but were forced to come at him singly due to the tight confines of the alley. With shreds of grime-stained skin and rotten nails hanging from his fingers, the first one to reach Alec thrust out another improvised polearm. Strapped to the business end was a cleaver, held in place with thongs of leather.

Alec flattened himself against the wall and felt the edge of the rusty blade slide over his jacket, barely scratching the leather. He caught the haft and brought his free elbow into the man's throat, feeling the windpipe collapse with the force of the blow. His attacker released his weapon and staggered back, gasping for air that would never reach his lungs.

With practiced ease, Alec spun the weapon and brought the cleaver crashing down on the charging clown. Despite the dullness and corrosion of the blade, the metal edge cracked the man's skull as if it were a rotten egg.

It was over before Alec had even broken a sweat. He stepped around the grimy man, who clutched at his broken airway as his face turned blue, and over the painted corpse, which still jerked spasmodically in a gross imitation of life. He walked past the glowing man with shards of glass puncturing his blood-streaked face. Finally, Alec approached the woman.

The song in his head had reached its natural end.

She appeared to be young, in her late teens or early twenties. The skirt she wore was long and split down the center, and her pale legs spilled from the material as she writhed in agony. Her tall crimson boots ground against the asphalt, soaked with the blood that had begun to pool from her wounds. As her dark corset rose and fell with each panicked and desperate breath, Alec noticed that the exposed flesh of her upper body was adorned with tattoos and piercings. Her hair, which looked to have been redyed so often that Alec could not guess at its original color, had begun to collect trash and debris.

Gathering her gently into his arms, Alec cooed, "It's okay." She was light to him, almost weightless.

She parted her lips with a sigh. Black ink stained her mouth, dissolving into a flock of birds that seemed to soar towards one ear. She whispered, "Do not leave me alone."

*   *   *

Her eyes snapped open. For a moment, the irises were lost in an inky blackness as deep as the pitch of night, but they returned quickly to the violet hue they had once been.

She was no longer in the streets, but lying on an unfamiliar bed consisting of cream-colored plastic and a soft mattress with an elevated head. Coarse sheets covered her from toe to shoulder, leaving only one arm and her head exposed. From her free limb ran a thin tube connected to a machine, above which hung a half-empty bag of liquids.

"Don't worry. You're safe." A voice barely louder than a whisper filled the room. Her rescuer was tall, thin, and wiry, and his short brown hair was unkempt and stood out against his pale flesh. Piercing green eyes met hers.

"This is for the pain." His voice came in a flat monotone as he unhooked her from the machine long enough to inject a syringe into the tube. The contents burned.

She sat up as he offered her a cup of water, letting the sheets slide down. Bandages had been wrapped skillfully about her chest and shoulder, but either side, ankhs, crosses, stars, moons, and other symbols mundane and foreign were etched everywhere on her skin.

"Thank you," she said, taking the cup. "Where am I?"

"*Hôpital du Sacré-Cœur de Montréal.*" The words rolled off her host's tongue with ease, demonstrating a familiarity with the language. "Welcome to my workplace."

"You're a healer?" she asked, remembering even through the haze of injury how quickly and easily he had dispatched of the men in the alley.

"I was once someone who chanted *Militi Succurrimus.*" When his words drew a blank stare, he added, "I was a medical technician. Now, I sweep the floors."

The painkillers had begun to take effect, and she was surprised to note that they did not cloud her mind but occluded the pain of her wounds. A cart rattled past the room, echoing as it journeyed down the hallway. Voices leached through the open door, but no one disturbed them. "Then I thank you for your help," she said, staring into the cup as one hand brushed the choker around her neck, rattling the runes hanging from it, "but you should let me be."

"If I knew that there was someone to tend to you, I would," her host explained, "but ever since I discovered you, it's like I've been invisible."

Blood rushed to her face, but she asked him to explain, even though she feared she knew what he meant.

"From the moment I picked you up, I've been ignored. Cars and pedestrians passed us by despite the fact that you were bleeding and unconscious. When I entered the emergency room, no one gave us a sideways glance. Nobody stopped me when I stole an empty bed and wheeled you in here, and even out of uniform, I was able to raid the tools and equipment without being accosted." Pausing, he sipped from his own cup before he asked, "What is going on?"

"You would not believe me," she whispered.

"I killed three men for you tonight! I think I'm owed an explanation," her rescuer snapped.

"My name is Veleda, and I am of the house of Neviah." Sadness laced her voice. "I am a Seer, a seeker of truth, and a teller of lies. I am both a princess and a peon. You should leave me be, and forget about me before you risk falling from reality and losing your place here forever."

"The blood of three people stains my hands tonight," her rescuer replied calmly, "and it's not like I have much to lose."

"They were riffraff, and will not be missed. Their bodies will turn to dust where they lay, and your authorities will never even notice them." Veleda spoke earnestly now. "As long as you are attached to me, you will not belong here. I am not of this realm."

The man crossed his arms; seeming so patient he would have waited an eternity for her to continue.

"We come from another world. We come from the dreamscape."

He stared at her, the word meaningless to him.

"When you rescued me, you joined the façade; the illusion that separates our worlds. Now you are hidden behind its veil. You can walk through a crowd and be ignored by all but those who've surrendered to it. At this moment, you do not exist."

"Then how did you see me?" he asked, doubt heavy in his voice.

"I...breached the façade to call for help," she answered warily, "and now I've dragged you between worlds. I'm sorry, I know it's hard to believe. If you take me back to where you found me, I can show you just how real the dreamscape is. But if I do so..." she trailed off.

Tossing his empty cup into the trash, her host lifted her corset from the sink, where it had been hanging to dry.

"Your shirt was ruined. Will you be okay with a gown instead?"

The bloodied shirt was stiff with dried fluids, and the gap where the pike bit her flesh had widened on the journey to the hospital. The garment her rescuer offered in its stead was a light blue short-sleeve robe that tied at the back.

"Does none of this bother you?" she asked.

"That's like asking a fish if it has trouble breathing underwater, or a bird if it can fly. To others the very concept is bizarre, but the fish and the bird simply do. I have seen so much, and still see so much, that being attacked by a psychotic clown, a glowing man, and that filthy cretin was not startling."

He shrugged. "To answer your question: no, I'm not bothered. In fact, I'm intrigued. I have nothing here to hold me back."

Falling silent, he offered the gown once more.

"Well," Veleda said, stretching out her hands to expose the myriad of tattoos and piercings that ran over them. "It's not my colour, but…"

Her guardian laughed as he slid the gown over her bandaged chest.

*　*　*

Where the three bodies had once been, there were now three piles of dust. Alec bent down and ran his fingers through the remains as the wind blew, further removing the evidence of the deaths. Even their weapons were gone, rusted away into nothing in a matter of hours.

"They were worth less than dust." Veleda said softly. "In death, they have improved by far."

"While I don't doubt that, I cannot help but wonder why they were attacking you." Alec stood, rubbing his hands together to remove the last traces of death from his fingers and cast it to the wind.

"I am wanted by my home's imposter king," she answered. "Fear and hatred are his methods; violence and death his tools."

"And what did you do to earn his ire?" Alec asked.

Veleda shivered as she answered, "He delights in prophecies. Hearing of my talents, he called me forth. Unlike others who sang falsely of his glory, I saw what was underneath. I understood his origin, and in doing so, incurred his wrath."

"So you fled here," Alec guessed.

"And found you," Veleda sighed.

"I'm a temporary saviour, at best." His voice was subdued. He almost sounded guilty. "What now?"

Veleda approached the image of a door that had been painted in abstract shapes and startling colors, sharply contrasting the drab bricks. "Here, a child dreamed of being an artist, and his inspiration carved a portal between our worlds. Here is where I crossed, where I was pursued and injured, and where I tore the façade open enough for you to peer inside. If you leave me now, you will once more be anchored to your world, but you will also be hunted. Cross with me, and you risk being forever lost."

The pill in Alec's pocket suddenly felt like a lead shot. Society would not miss him, nor wonder where he had gone. He had nothing here; nobody to mourn him, no pet to feed, and no valuables save the few medals of valor that had once labeled him a hero, but now collected dust in a cupboard.

There was no decision to be made.

Smiling at the chance to return to duty, Alec walked through the doorway.

CHAPTER 2

Had he been forewarned about the effects of crossing over, he may well have reconsidered. So intense were the nausea, vertigo, and dysphoria that hit him as he crossed, Alec collapsed to his hands and knees, gagging on air that felt too thick to swallow.

The buildings about him that had once been rigid structures of brick, mortar, and concrete, were now composed of mysterious materials festooned with sculptures of hideous creatures. Lines that had once been parallel and perpendicular were now twisted and corkscrewed, and plain windows were now adorned in myriad colors and abstract patterns.

The sky, formerly filled with clouds and glowing yellow from the city lights, was now a kaleidoscope of shifting purple hues and pitch darkness; sometimes glowing, sometimes devouring all illumination. Dirigibles, autogyros, and flying beasts soared overhead.

"Be still, Alec." Veleda advised from where she sat. The poured-asphalt alleyway beneath her was now a hodgepodge of cobbled stone and brick. "Your mind must adjust to this reality. You normally venture here only in your subconscious, and being here in a wakened state has driven lesser men mad."

"Thank you...for the warning," he gasped, breathing in odd yet strangely familiar scents. It was as if he could smell bread baking, but the flour was off, and he could taste the bizarre color the loaf would become. Alec rolled onto his back and saw that naked fires now pulsed and flickered in place of the streetlights as if they were untamed beasts, writhing with a life of their own.

Determined to conquer his pain, Alec pulled himself to his feet. The pulse in his ears beat slowly, then accelerated, only to cease entirely before starting again. His mouth filled with the flavors of burnt ash and seared metal, and distant shadows stopped, sped up and slowed back down of their own accord. Around him, one person became two, and they merged into an amorphous blob, suddenly becoming no more than a slick and streamlined blur. Unable to endure the assault on his senses, Alec stumbled against a wall, gripping it as a man afraid of heights might have clutched a balcony railing.

"You come from Banality." Veleda explained. "We are now in the realm of magic, faith, and wishes. In this age of enlightenment, your people choose to forgo a part of your world by blinding themselves with science and reason. This land endured in the shadows, and exists as a pillar of all hopes, aspirations, fantasies, and nightmares."

Through his palms, Alec felt a heartbeat that was not his own. "Your world…"

"Lives and breathes on the back of yours," his charge smiled. "While itself remaining distinct and individual."

Closing his eyes, Alec concentrated on the warm stone against his cheek. It seemed vibrant; aware of his presence, even. The sights, sounds, and smells that had tortured him melted away like a cube of ice left in the sun; finally evaporating into a steady placidity that sang a gentle harmony from the depths of the world through the stone to soothe his ragged nerves.

Struggling to his feet, he fought with himself as the distant music disappeared. As much as Alec wanted to hear it again, his sense of responsibility could no longer be ignored. Blood had broken through Veleda's bandages, becoming a stark reminder of more urgent matters.

Alec and Veleda stepped from the alley into the street. There were people in all manner of odd dress ranging from medieval tunics to Victorian era suits; heads topped with ancient helmets or colonial hats. Some of the people had robotic limbs and bionic implants, while others bore inhuman alien tentacles. They were adorned in everything from opulent finery to nothing at all, in fashions both conservative and erotic. A carriage drawn by dark shadows consumed by flame careened down the street, followed by a fancy car that screamed excess income and wealth, and trailed by a skeleton on a penny-wheel. Having become used to being ignored, Alec started when everyone turned to stare at him with a look of dread and reverence.

"To the hospital, please, Alec." Veleda reminded him, laying a gentle hand on his shoulder. Casting aside all cares, he hailed down a king-sized bed that galloped upon the eight hairy legs of a spider. The driver, a young boy dressed in a princess costume, and his companion, a lady garbed in a cape and tights, stared awkwardly as Veleda was lowered gently onto the mattress.

*   *   *

The automatic sliding doors of the hospital were now wrought iron gates that contorted and pulled themselves wide enough apart for the two to pass. The linoleum within had transformed into polished sandstone, and the beds were still familiar wheeled contrivances, but they were no longer built of white plastic and stainless steel. Instead, they were made of ornately carved and lacquered wood adorned with brass fittings.

There was no reception desk or triage nurse. Instead, Veleda reached into a dispenser with an outstretched hand, and a stone marble rolled down a complex track to land softly on her palm. She seemed to relax as Alec lowered her onto an ornate bench carved with images of rebirth and snakes shedding their skins.

Try as he might, Alec could not stop staring at a figure cleaning the floors by directing autonomous brooms with what seemed to be a magic wand. He recognized the man. Unlike the straight and proud position his peer normally adopted, the person in front of him was pale, rakish, and stooped. Instead of wearing scrubs, he was dressed in a transparent mesh shirt. An inverted cross was burned into the flesh over his heart.

A hand closed over Alec's arm, and Veleda looked at him with concern.

"I'm sorry." Alec apologized, finally looking away from the person he had been studying. "It's just that I work with this man."

Veleda's frown was small and sad. "No, you don't. You may work with his *Crafter*, but he whom you see there is a doppelgänger, a dream-form created from the fantasies of your world. Every time a human is born, a shadow of the original is created here and fed by your world's dreams. If the Crafter dies," she paused to shrug, "the doppelgänger merely continues in this world, but if the dream-form dies, the Crafter suffers. The loss of the ability to dream has led many on your side to go insane. Sometimes, new dream-forms can be created, but often the loss of a doppelgänger leads to tragedy."

"And what of you?" Alec asked. "Are you a dream-form?"

"No." Veleda laughed quietly, her voice pleasant. "I am original to this plane, a dream-walker. We are ones who are born from union in this land. My mother was a dream-form, but my father is like me, born from a relationship within this realm. We are tied to the dreamscape, yet we can escape it as well. That's why I was able to enter your world."

"Do I have a doppelgänger?" Alec wondered. Before she could answer, the stone in Veleda's hand glowed.

*   *   *

The multiple pairs of glasses that the doctor wore turned his eyes into mountains that could reach the heavens from even the flattest planes. They helped him zero in on what he needed to see, but did nothing to hide the grotesque detail of the orbs from anyone who looked at them.

Beckoning her to sit upon a bed adorned with more ornate carvings, he pulled aside the bandage on Veleda's leg, hemming and hawing to himself as he inspected the dressing.

"Immaculate work. Yes, it truly is." The doctor murmured to himself. "Efficient compression while leaving a path for drainage; wound has been cleaned with acids and bases and salts and water. It's a stunning job, done, no doubt, by an experienced professional. My compliments to the dresser."

Alec remained silent as the doctor studied the wound. He was old and bent nearly double, with a white beard and wild unkempt hair. His clothes were faded and weatherworn, and the many buckles of his jacket were scratched and fatigued. His apron was dark leather, better suited to a blacksmith than a man of medicine.

"You, lad, come over and apply pressure to the leg here!" the doctor shouted at Alec.

Alec grabbed Veleda's limb where indicated, noticing for a second the softness of the pliable muscle underneath her flesh before his calloused hand clamped down, limiting the flow of blood.

"That is odd," the doctor observed, suddenly more interested in Alec than his patient. "You are dressed unusually; rugged, yet so plain. You must have one truly unimaginative Crafter, no?"

As suddenly as he had asked, the doctor was busy again, distracted by his work. Looking away from the man, Alec met eyes with Veleda, who smiled at him in silent understanding.

"While I'm searching for the right herbs, would you clean the wound, young sir?" the doctor asked, handing Alec a bowl and rags before hurrying off to crush a series of seemingly random spices together within a mortar and pestle.

Alec obeyed, cleaning the wound with gentle but firm swipes.

"Good job, lad!" the doctor exclaimed as he returned and dumped the entire contents into the wound. "You've done this many a time before, I see."

Beginning to mix another batch, he stopped midway to look at Alec with more scrutiny. "You look familiar, for an oddball."

"He gets that a lot." Veleda said softly.

"Right, right, of course he does. Pull back that bandage on her shoulder there, thanks."

The same treatment was applied, and without another word, the doctor turned and left the room.

Lowering herself from the bed, Veleda tested her leg and rotated her arm.

"Is it wise to move so soon?" her guardian wondered aloud.

"The wound is closed and numb now. A gift of this land's magic—I heal faster than you, but not as well as a doppelgänger. They can recover from fatal wounds within hours.

"But you said they can die?"

"By the right hand or under the right influence, yes, but rarely by their own stupidity or at the hands of another of their kind." Placing a hand on Alec's chest, Veleda shivered. "For all their strengths, they are extremely malleable under the touch of others."

Pursing his lips, Alec nodded. "So a lethal blow from me..."

"What you can create, you can destroy," she answered, standing tall. "That is something that cannot be altered in this realm, regardless of your Banality or Fancy."

After a slow breath, Alec flexed his hands and asked, "What now?"

"Perhaps we should head somewhere less conspicuous? Your Banality is obvious, and is drawing much attention."

She was right. No matter where Alec looked, people were staring, and the attention made him very uncomfortable.

Taking her hand, he let Veleda lead him through the crowded hospital, and out into the absurdity of the streets.

Alec tried to avoid the inhabitants of them, but shadows plagued him. Silhouettes flitted among the crowds, and dark outlines of people, pets, and wildlife were visible wherever he looked. He took great pains to avoid the mysterious shapes until he realised no one else around him paid them heed. Losing concentration long enough to barge through one, he was surprised to feel nothing. He stood there in bewilderment before urgently calling out Veleda's name.

She listened as he quietly explained what had happened, and nodded. "It is good that you see the shadows of the other realm; it means you are not lost from it. As long as you are still connected to the other side, you can return; if you wish."

"This will fade in time?" Alec's eyes followed a rather appealing shadow, but Veleda didn't seem to notice, or see the entity.

"Unless you have a way to separate yourself from the dreaming, yes, you will lose your Banality. As you gather wonder, the other side will become a false reality."

Alec bid her to continue the journey with a nod, but when her back was turned, he hesitated long enough to shake the bottle in his pocket, listening for the reassuring rattle of the solitary pill inside. Strangely comforted by its presence when it came, he followed her.

A great globe crested the horizon, its mass composed of swirling whites, oranges, violets, and brilliant yellows. As its light spilled across the land, it pierced Alec's eyes, rang through his head, and brought agonies anew. Stumbling, he stopped to catch his breath.

They were only paces from a park. Exhausted, he leaned against a sapling, and the melodies he had pined for once more filled his head, growing louder and sweeter whenever he looked in their source's direction.

If Veleda spoke to him, he did not hear her. Stumbling forward, he found the cobblestone replaced by luscious grass, soft and tender. The woods about him sang beautiful melodies that sapped his strength and soothed his skull.

Unable to support himself any longer, Alec collapsed. He closed his eyes, and under the sweet songs of lullabies, drifted off to sleep.

*   *   *

The great globe was directly overhead, peaked at its zenith. It burned through the thin skin of his eyelids, dragging him from his blissful slumber and back into the dream-realm.

Where he expected to feel chills, Alec found warmth. The ground beneath him was not wet, but soft and forgiving. The sounds of traffic and the cacophony of the city were gone, replaced with the lilting harmonies of the trees rustling and the twittering of wildlife.

He heard a splash of water, and turned his head to find Veleda kneeling by a crystal-clear pool. Her robes were lowered from her chest, and now her bandages had been removed, Alec could see more of the strange symbols across her skin. His eyes traced the swell of her chest along the patterns until the robe obscured the remaining artwork and the forbidden flesh. She had been washing her hair. As he gazed at her, she rinsed it, squeezed it dry, and began to comb it with her fingers.

"Isn't it strange that we can be so relaxed in the middle of a metropolis?" The coarseness of his voice surprised Alec as he pulled himself to his feet and limped to the water's edge.

"We aren't in the city anymore." Veleda corrected. "These are wandering woods. If you show them respect and care, you can journey freely from one land to the next through them."

"And what of those who lack respect?" Alec asked.

"They will find their destination to be far more permanent and unpleasant than desired."

"I, see," he said warily, patting the exposed root of a grand willow gratefully. "Thank you," he whispered, and it rustled in response.

When he laughed at the reply, it was the sound of dry grass blowing in a midsummer breeze. "Is there a place to drink?" Alec coughed.

Twisting her hair tightly, Veleda indicated a burbling spring that fed the pond. Parched, Alec slipped his face into the stream and sucked greedily. It was sweet, fresh, and peppery. It satisfied his thirst, but failed to satiate his hunger. He had not eaten since the day before, and after the exhausting night, he was famished. While he continued to drink, he grew suddenly disoriented as his ears filled with the sounds of rushing water.

He pulled his face from the pool and saw the world spinning from side to side. It was as if he was back in the desert. Explosions battered his senses, rattled his teeth, and boomed in his skull. The world before his eyes stretched and skewed, and the music was replaced with the buzz of bullets, the cries of the dying, and the all too familiar sounds of carnage and chaos.

Clutching desperately to the grass, Alec prayed for the memories to cease.

"How far from wonder have you gone?" Veleda's voice sang from far away. "When was the last time you allowed yourself to dream?"

A bottle pressed against his side.

"You are drunk on this realm," her voice explained, rubbing his shoulders and back. "Your body is rejecting what you refuse to believe exists."

"I am here!" He gasped

"But you are not believing the existence of the dreamscape at your core."

"I am here!" he yelled, pinching his neck hard enough to draw blood. When he did not find himself awakening in his bed or hungover on a cheaply-tiled floor, his head cleared and the ground stopped shifting.

Still unsteady, Alec stood; snapping to attention, his body locked into a forced rigidity. He did not blink, did not flinch. Another familiar song rang out in this head, this one asking a single question. "Where is my mind?" he asked, quoting the lyric aloud.

Closing his eyes, he fought to push away the acrid smell of gunpowder, the coppery taste of blood, the screams of the dying, the pain of old wounds, and the visions of long-lost comrades.

"I am here," he said again, and he was back in the wandering glen, the music of the trees once more blessing his ears.

Suddenly calm, confident, and in control, Alec turned to his concerned companion.

"So, where are we wandering to?"

CHAPTER 3

"This is a dangerous and ill-thought out idea." Alec exclaimed, one hand tightly clenched around the stout staff the woods had gifted him. "If your pursuers have any sense, they will be waiting for us here."

Downcast but determined, Veleda stepped from the copse onto her family's land. Wherever they were, the area was not unfamiliar to Alec. The cold air left the ground hard and brittle with frost, while a lake of fire burned nearby and a pond of glass shimmered across the lot. The flat roofed buildings seemed to indicate a milder climate, despite the bitter chill.

Shrugging, Alec followed his charge. He paused as a two-headed goat trotted across his path, bleating and leaping before it disappeared into a bramble. Marching silhouettes still crossed his path, but they weren't quite as difficult to ignore, and Alec wondered if they had faded a little in his eyes.

As the music of the glen vanished, Alec felt on edge, but Veleda seemed happy, yet nervous. "This way," she indicated, ducking between two multi-colored shacks and darting through the shadows between them. They crossed through two yards fenced in stone and clay. Emerging from a narrow ditch, Alec saw a three story circular building that had a domed roof and was surrounded by outbuildings, stables, and a barn.

Although Veleda had led them this far, Alec now took the lead as they entered the main building and found themselves lost among paintings and murals.

When they reached it, the kitchen was a disaster. Pots, pans, cutlery, and utensils littered the floor or lay haphazardly on the counters and benches. Broken ceramics crunched underfoot, and furniture was dented or smashed as if seized by a giant's hands. Examining a pot that lay by the oven, Alec was relieved to see the rings of hardened minerals that indicated hours of rest and evaporation.

Sliding past her guardian, Veleda hurried through a door on the other side of the kitchen. Alec hurriedly pulled a cleaver free from the plaster wall and followed.

Twists and turns down serpentine corridors that seemed as though they had been chiseled from one giant log left Alec feeling dazed. Clay and cast-iron figurines, curtains of gemstone and silk, surreal frescoes, and tapestries woven from spider webs all played with his eyes as he charged ahead at a dead sprint; desperate to keep Veleda in view. Finally, they emerged from the passage.

He only had a moment to take in the giant leaves, long petrified by age and shimmering as if crystalline, that formed the arching ceiling. Around him, the great room was filled with a knotted and aged tree, which seemed to breathe, sing, and glow all at once. The air was fresh and moist, sliding comfortably into Alec's lungs as he caught his breath.

Veleda was by the great trunk, her arms were outstretched, and the smile she wore was one of bliss and contentment. It was the look of an addict getting her next hit, a babe finally realizing the voice she heard was her mother's, or the look of a bride walking down the aisle.

"Mistress!" someone shouted. Alec shifted his weight, and the heavy blade of a cutlass sliced through the air, barely missing his head. Bringing his right arm into play, the stout staff he still carried crashed into the face of an anthropomorphic lamb, knocking the first of his several attackers senseless.

Alec blocked a descending wood axe from another with the staff before the cleaver he carried bit deeply between the new attacker's shoulder and body.

A scraggily-dressed knave followed, wielding a dark onyx blade ornately touched with gold and swinging from below. For a third time, the staff parried the jab. Alec released the wood and caught the attacker's wrist with both hands.

"Don't"

Veleda's voice was loud and desperate, but the pulse beating in his ears rendered Alec practically deaf, even as he bent the knave's wrists inwards, pulling him off balance.

"Kill"

Memories flooded back. He was beating the young mugger who had dared to rob him, grabbing the youth by the throat. He was in the house, struggling with an insurgent who had just tried to disembowel him with a dagger while Sylvain, Frederick, and Kiso hurried to help—

Shooting forward, Alec wrapped his fingers around his attacker's windpipe. He squeezed, the muscles in his arm flexing as he prepared for the motion that would snap the neck.

"Them!"

Then he was Alec again, and he knew what he had to do. The attackers were not professional warriors; they were farmers, workers, and servants. A push-kick slammed the knave against the wall where he sagged, stunned into silence.

All but one of the remaining mob hesitated. A thin, smoke-shrouded wraith dressed in dark robes that absorbed the surrounding light advanced.

Grinning, Alec ran forward. Just before they collided, he ducked and rolled, disappearing into the swirling mists. He emerged from the maelstrom on his toes. His hand shot out and clutched the living shadow's throat. Lifting the figure off its feet with one hand, he blocked the thrust of a thin blade with his free hand. Alec twisted and slammed his opponent into the unforgiving wooden floor. Stunned, the dark one released its blades, and the onyx swords rattled away. Their clattering was the only sound in the room.

Grabbing the figure's hood, Alec exposed the face of his opponent. Her dark skin was almost as black as the cloak she wore, but was lighter than the tattoo whose curved lines wrapped around her features, crossing over her high cheekbones, across her long, narrow nose, around her dark brown eyes, and up to the braided hair that was pulled tight across her scalp.

Twin lines ran parallel down her face from her forehead to her lips.

Turning her head away from Alec's piercing gaze, his opponent looked into Veleda's violet orbs. She spoke in a voice that was deep and smooth, and carried an accent that Alec could not identify. She whispered, yet it seemed to echo about the room. "Welcome home, mistress."

"M'lanth!" Veleda cried in relief.

Releasing his hold, Alec stood and extended his hand to his defeated foe. When she took the offering of peace, her sleeve fell back to reveal arcane glowing tattoos that started just after her wrist and continued all of the way up her arm. She was light, weighing almost nothing in his hold, but she found her footing without issue, and her bare feet seemed to hold the ground as if she were welded to it.

As the dark warrior embraced the Seer, Alec brushed dust from his pants and chuckled. "I assume you two are friends?"

No one shared his humor, and a small collection of servants murmured beneath their breaths and stared at Alec in horror. Pointing into the masses, Alec demanded a translation.

"They say you are 'him'," someone called from the crowd.

"Who's 'him?'" Alec snapped back.

"It's not," another voice joined the fray. "He moves differently, and he's skinnier."

"Who is 'him'?!" Alec yelled.

"Tend to the wounded." M'lanth ordered.

Veleda knelt near the one whom Alec had hacked with the cleaver and cried out, "Find a doctor! He's been hurt by a Crafter."

The crowd pulled back in fear. Some threw themselves against the farthest walls, while others performed whatever gestures were relevant to invoke the mercy of their deity. Some even hid their faces or stared in reverence.

"Hurry!" M'lanth's cry caused a rush of activity.

Guilt flowed through Alec's heart as he watched the wounded being carted away, but then his soul hardened. They had attacked him first; he had only been defending himself.

M'lanth spoke to the remaining mob, "I want a perimeter formed in case any of the unbound king's goons show up."

Everyone scrambled to follow her orders except the one whose blade Alec had taken. The knave came forward to claim it, but shifting his weight, Alec leveled the knife at the man's throat.

"Victor's spoils," he growled.

When the knave seemed fit to protest, M'lanth silenced any objection.

"You were useless with that blade, K'tath." She reminded the peasant. "If you take back your dagger, you can come with us, but you will die, and he will claim it as his own then anyway."

Shrinking against the threat, the man retreated alongside the other peasants and farmers who hurried to their duties. Plucking up the scabbard that the knave had hurriedly left for him, Alec secured his weapon and walked back to the two women, who chatted quietly by the roots of the gigantic tree.

"You should not have come back." M'lanth spoke in her crystalline voice. "But I'm glad you did."

"It's not for long." Veleda replied. "We've just come to get supplies."

"Let's hurry, then." M'lanth moved forward as if to guide Veleda from the room. Unwilling to let her take Veleda out of his sight, Alec blocked her path, one hand on his appropriated blade. Both fighters remained seemingly relaxed, but they sized each other up nevertheless. The earlier battle may have ended in Alec's favor, but he was certain that M'lanth had not revealed all of her tricks.

"Stand down," the woman insisted. "No harm will come to our Lady in my presence."

Alec tensed. I

t was as close to saying 'move it or lose it' as she was going to get.

"We will be fine, Alec. My shadow-knight and I will return in moments." Veleda reassured her companion. "Please, make yourself at home."

With those words, M'lanth brushed past Alec as if he were little more than an idle statue, and focused her attention back towards Veleda.

"Your family…" the warrior began.

"I know." Veleda answered sadly, presumably interrupting so she did not have to relive whatever horrors she had already endured.

Then they were gone.

Left alone, Alec rested his back against the giant tree. Once more, the beat of the dreamscape filled his head. Closing his eyes, he lifted his arms and welcomed the beauty of it into his soul. The music he heard was the sound of a thousand chimes singing gently across a faraway plain. Alongside the crystal whispers was a deep and resonant beat, slightly slower than that of his heart. It rose and fell gently with each breath, pulsing in his ears and chest. He could almost taste the tranquility. His ears *felt*—not heard—the shifting tones, and his very muscles trembled with each throb.

Then it was over, interrupted by the return of his companions. Veleda had changed her leggings and had replaced her beaten top; M'lanth held a new bundle of gear in her arms.

With an underhand toss, she threw a ration pack to Alec. He caught it one-handed, and she ordered, "Eat and gain strength, guardian."

"Guardian?" he asked.
"Have you not protected our Lady thus far?"
"I have."
"Then," M'lanth turned back to her preparations, "you are her guardian."

Alec processed this for a moment, then shrugged and unwrapped the meal. She was right; he supposed as he bit into the soft, buttery pastry filled with meat and vegetables, he had taken up the role without much thought. To hear it aloud renewed his determination.

Once he had finished his food, Alec looked at the shadow-knight and nodded his thanks.
"So, you travel with us?"

Momentarily disappearing from the room and returning with a rucksack, Veleda tossed it to her newly appointed guardian. "M'lanth will accompany us. We will appreciate her presence."

"Where to now?" he asked, adjusting the weight of the bag on his back that he was still free to fight and draw his new blade.

"Back to the forest." M'lanth answered. "And onward from there."

The two warriors prepared to leave, but stopped when the woman they had both sworn to protect failed to follow. Looking at Alec, M'lanth nodded to indicate he should talk to Veleda. Stepping softly, he returned to his charge's side.

"This is your house?" Alec asked in awe.

"Kind of," Veleda answered. "The top floor of our community hall belongs to my blood, and the other floors belong to my second uncle and my distant cousin, but it's all been ransacked an no one's home. None of my family is here."

Her hands clenched until her vermillion nails pierced her palms. Crimson blood trickled over her pale skin in an outward sign of the force of her emotions.

"A long time ago, my ancestors fed the viewing tree their life-force when it was time to move on from this realm. In time, it came to give us this home. Since our blood was infused with it, the tree became a magnifier for our powers. It is so connected to us that we learn to talk to it when we're born."

"What's it saying to you now?" Alec asked.

"It's lonely." Veleda responded with a sigh. She closed her eyes and laid one slender hand against the trunk of the tree. Alec watched as rivulets of blood ran down the grooves in the rough bark. At that moment, the room seemed to grow more vibrant and energetic. When he looked back at her again, the smile she wore reminded Alec of a wolf about to consume its prey.

"And it's my duty to bring *our* family back."

CHAPTER 4

The fields were empty as they passed the houses on their way back to the glen, and Alec saw no one, but felt as though they were being watched. At first, he assumed it was the villagers on guard, but as he set foot on the grassy field, sorrowful trumpeting rang out from the trees.

Loosening her blades from their scabbards, M'lanth let her cloak swirl into vapor, covering most of her body in shadows.

Taking note, Alec prepared to draw his blade as surreptitiously as he could.

"Who waits for us?" the shadow-knight asked of the Seer. "The caution comes from the glen itself."

In answer, Veleda winked at Alec, wearing a mirthless smile. "Due to my ancestry, the wandering field is on our side. You wished to know what happened to those who disrespected the trees? They are asking you to give them fertilizer for their roots."

"And who are we to deny such a request?" The shadow-knight's smile reminded Alec of a snake before it strikes. As the swirling mist overcame her, she vanished into the woods.

Stepping off the beaten path and into the moss and trees, Alec approached the glen. Veleda walked directly down the path as an easy target, hammering her heels into the earth and forcing the dozen enemy troops ahead to take notice.

"Welcome back, Seer of Neviah," one of the soldiers sneered. He was part man and part machine. The wires that hung from his head glistened and glowed in a kind of Morse code that symbolized the transfer of data. His eyes were lenses, constantly shifting as they adjusted to his surroundings. His body was armored in beige plastic and metal and cooled by grilled fans that hummed softly.

"Your Lord and Master wishes to have a word with you," sneered a man in a pristine business suit as he stepped around the machine man. Removing his sunglasses to clean them, he exposed empty sockets, through which a red light glowed from the very back of his skull.

"He is not, and never will be, *my* Lord," Veleda hissed.

"He is this land's ruler…" the man in the suit began.

"This land's *disputed* ruler," she countered, jutting her chin forward.

The machine man began to argue, but stopped himself. His head jerked from side to side spasmodically as the lenses whirred to focus on something distant. "She's not alone." Training the lenses directly on where Alec hid, the cyborg hissed. It sounded more like the screeching of an old modem than a noise any biological being could make.

"You *have* delivered after all," the eyeless one laughed. His chuckle sounded like dry leaves being crushed.

"Do not jump to conclusions," The man of flesh and machine sounded tinny, as if he had entirely surrendered to his robotic side. "Data insufficient. I cannot provide a positive ID."

Only the apparent leader remained fixated on the Seer now. The rest spread into a circle, weapons ready and staring into the bush.

"Reveal yourself," said a knight whose onyx armor seemed to be hammered into his flesh. The exposed edges of his skin oozed with pus and ichor. "Or our captive dies." Alec saw a gaunt figure standing beside the armored behemoth, a rope wrapped around their neck.

"*Va chier*! Go to shit!" Alec responded, refusing the dark knight's demand.

Unamused at such an unhelpful reply, the eyeless one casually waved a hand towards the knight.

Wrenching the noose tighter around the captive's neck, the dark knight forced the figure to his knees. Despite the fibers biting into the flesh of his throat, the prisoner looked Veleda in the eyes and rasped out, "Run!"

Alex felt a rare moment of concern as he recognized the man's face.

In the realm of Banality, Frederick was a shell of a man; rarely conscious and barely alive. A buried bomb had cost him the use of his legs, and flames from the blast had melted his skin, seared his lungs, and left him in constant agony. In the other realm, he spent his days in a drug-induced haze. Between rare moments of lucidity, he mumbled of faraway lands and sights beyond description.

Frederick's ramblings finally made sense; he had been trying to tell Alec of his doppelgänger's adventures. It was little wonder that he had chosen bedlam over Banality. Gone were the scars, replaced with healthy glowing skin. His wasted and atrophied limbs now twitched with barely restrained energy, and his eyes, once dulled by drugs and pain, now glimmered vibrantly.

"I swear to you bastards," Alec's voice echoed off the surrounding trees. "If any of you bring harm to him, I will send you to Hell."

Emitting a mechanical sound that might have been a laugh, the machine man turned with one hand raised.

The stone that thudded against the mechanical man's head was small but fast, and from the wound poured numbers, letters, and symbols that coursed down his neck.

Snarling, the man in the suit tore off his glasses and sought out the origin of the projectile, only for a flying sword to cleave his head in two. The heavy blade split his face vertically as it dug deep through flesh and bone. He fumbled desperately with both hands to push his head back together before falling to the soft grass.

Desperate to save his friend, Alec rushed forward from his cover as the dark knight brought his blade down towards Frederick's neck. He knew he would be too late even as he charged.

Suddenly, an unusually supple maple branch wrapped around the knight's sword arm and yanked him from his feet, flinging him into the pond, where the heavy armor he wore dragged him to the bottom.

Laughing at the confusion that spread across the enemy ranks as they stared after him, Veleda jeered, "Even the land refuses your leader's sovereignty."

Alec's charge continued, bringing him near to the still-dazed machine man. Gripping his dagger with both hands, he severed the thing's head from the body. Robotic hands clasped the gaping stump in a futile attempt to stem the flow of data, until the headless corpse stumbled, fell backwards, and finally lay still in a growing pool of letters and numbers.

In the center of the melee, there came a roar of pain and rage as a man in a silken suit swelled. Large limbs covered in dark, wiry fur ripped through flesh and cloth as his body split apart to reveal the monster inside. Opening its mouth, the giant bat-like beast grabbed Frederick, prepared to clamp its multitude of teeth over his shoulder and neck as the doppelgänger fought back against the creature's powerful grip.

Alec cried out to his friend and grabbed the beast's ear, driving his blade deep into the monster's skull, twisting the blade, and releasing his grip on the weapon only when the beast had slumped to the ground.

Yanking the blade free, Frederick sent it spinning into the chest of a young thug in a hoody who wielded a sharpened skateboard over his head. The knife cut into the lad's chest with such power that he flipped head over heels, striking the ground with a loud crack as his neck crumpled under the impact.

Alec turned, and was relieved to see that Veleda was safe. There were two broken bodies at her feet; the leaves jutting from them indicating death by topiary. Meanwhile,

M'lanth was running the last of her opponents through with her blade. She had single-handedly wiped out half of their foes.

Seeing that all was quiet, Alec turned to his friend and began to ask, "Are you oka—"

Grabbing Alec's cheeks, Frederick planted his lips over his friend's and kissed him with unrestrained passion. It was so unexpected that Alec froze, unsure of how to react.

It was Fred's doppelgänger who broke the kiss. Reaching out, he brushed hesitant fingers over Alec's face.

"Oh no." The doppelgänger blanched. "You're not a ghost."

"No, Fred. I am very much alive." Alec answered, his confusion obvious.

M'lanth walked over to them having collected her other sword. "Ghosts are fabrications of others that

Creators form in their sleep. Oftentimes, they don't survive if your kind disappear from their Creator's dreams."

"I understand." Alec said, biting his lip as a new thought occurred to him. "Wait. Fred, have you kissed ghosts of me before?"

Looking at his feet, the doppelgänger shuffled them and answered, "Maybe once or twice…a week." There was something different in his voice as he continued. "But I never thought you would find out. I'm trapped here because of the pain, and I knew I wouldn't ever meet your doppelgänger, so I thought I was safe to dream."

Catching Fred by his shoulders, Alec stared into his eyes. "Is this really you talking? You're not just his doppelgänger?"

"He is both." Veleda answered, having paid her respects to the glen for its assistance.

"How?" Alec asked.

"It's the drugs." Fred answered methodically. "I'm kept on such a strong cocktail of painkillers that I'm always asleep. I learned the truth during my surgeries. I was so far gone, so near death, that everything about this realm became clear."

The voice changed to the doppelgänger's again.

"And now my Creator is sharing space in my head. It's driving me crazy, which is really saying something, all things considered."

"Now," both voices merged as Fred's hands traveled up to Alec's shoulders. "How am I talking to you, if you're not a ghost?"

"I've entered the dreamscape."

A blush exploded across Frederick's face as Alec continued. "So, about that kiss?"

"You weren't supposed to know." Frederick admitted. "In our dreams, we can release our inhibitions, be who we truly wish to be, and live out our most taboo desires. We can remove our masks and reveal our true self. Ever since you first saved my life, I felt safe around you. It wasn't until I was dying that I realised why."

Frederick sighed as he tore his gaze from Alec's. "And by then, I knew you would never love me. I'm barely alive, just a slab of meat living vicariously in this world."

"Do you know I visited you more than once a month?" Alec asked.

"I thought that was a dream."

Alec chuckled as he patted his friend on the back, a sad smile on his face that Fred returned.

"If you two are done, we should not keep Mistress Veleda waiting." M'lanth was several paces ahead of them on the path, and her scowl was piercing.

"Of course," Alec agreed.

"Where were you heading?" Frederick asked.

"To the leaders who resist," the Seer declared. "It's time we changed the tides of this war."

"Mind if I tag along? I was going that way anyway." Fred's question was directed at Veleda, who bowed graciously and handed a spear from a fallen warrior to him in answer.

"Commander, it would be a pleasure," Veleda replied.

Alec's confused glance was greeted by only a shrug as M'lanth walked back down the path to fall into step behind the Seer and Frederick.

"Wait!" he yelled as he hurried after them. "Commander?"

CHAPTER 5

"Even here, I could not escape a war." Frederick admitted with regret as they walked further into the woods. "At least this time I know what I am fighting for."

"And what is that, exactly?" Alec asked, studying his friend.

"The right to dream. Our enemy already controls half the dreamscape, and those caught within his tyrannical hold are being groomed for war."

Alec cocked his head slightly, not understanding the implication of an army of doppelgängers in the dreamscape.

When Frederick spoke again, it was in the doppelgänger's voice alone. "You might not see it yet, but over the past few months, more and more people have endured nightly terrors and unrest."

"Frederick is awake, isn't he?" Alec asked

The shudder that ran through the doppelgänger's body was genuine. "We've become so interlinked that I feel his pain even when we're apart. His skin is constantly burning, and his legs feel tight and restless. If there was a way to change it or break the cycle, I would. Maybe when this war is over and the dreamscape is safe, we will choose a way to end our suffering, but until then," he shrugged, "we will fight on."

The sky shifted as they walked out of the woods, transforming from its mottled green hues to a golden glow that stirred memories Alec would rather suppress. It held the honey-colored touch of yellow sand thrown high in the sky in the remnants of a sandstorm.

No words were needed. Holding their weapons loosely, the trio of bodyguards formed a protective ring about the woman who had brought them together.

The scene about them was just one more abstract sight, but the dreamscape's version of the iconic New York skyline still gave Alec pause. It was partly occluded by the sand that blew through the colorless streets, having long ago scoured all surfaces clean of paint. Only the square patch of woodland behind them was untouched by the storm. In fact, it seemed to make great pains to avoid the centralized parkland as it continued to ravage elsewhere.

They paused at the edge of the blowing grit. Faces watched them from windows and doorways. The shadows of the other realm still hurried past, dancing haphazardly in the distance.

They were harder to see than before.

The bottle and its single pill felt heavy in Alec's pocket.

"Commander, is your Creator available?" "M'lanth asked.

Frederick's doppelgänger closed his eyes for a moment, and then replied, "Soon."

"May I enquire," Alec asked nervously, feeling very exposed with all the eyes upon them, "why we are waiting? The sands do not seem to be relenting."

"Nor will they," Veleda answered, passing her hand through the storm and bringing it back with a palm full of sand.

"Every grain is an idea born or a dream destroyed. For some time, the Sandmen tended and collected this by-product of imagination, but the enemy decided to imprison them. Without their assistance, the storms have grown in power and severity."

"The lands of the Resistance have suffered the worst." M'lanth continued. "Our cities have been affected most severely, but we adapt. As the land has become filled with storms, we have retreated to our subways, tunnels, and sewer systems."

"So those watching us…" Alec wondered.

"Are the tired, poor, and huddled masses yearning to breathe free from oppression once more. Most are displaced doppelgängers, severed from their Crafters by our foe's efforts."

"It is for them I fight." Frederick's own voice now flowed strongly from the lips of the doppelgänger. Winking at Alec, the veteran spread his arms, and his simple clothing suddenly transformed into an armored uniform covered in embroidered military insignia He had a Keffiyeh wound about his neck and face, leaving only his eyes uncovered.

"Neat trick," Alec said.

"Thank you." Frederick's reply was muffled. "As Creators, we have the power to shape this world. Try it yourself."

Alec closed his eyes and tried to will a scarf of his own into existence, yet when he opened his eyes, there was none. Noticing his confusion, Veleda, who was wrapping a fallen palm frond around her own face as she watched them, called out, "It may be your distance from our world."

There was no need to elaborate. The weight of the pill was enough to remind him of his ongoing connection to the banal world, even if he wanted to believe he was free of it now.

Alec removed his shirt and wrapped it around his head, exposing the thin and wiry body he had kept hidden until now, which was so lean his ribs protruded from the sides of a concave abdomen. He zipped his jacket up and nodded to the others. They had wasted enough time.

The sandstorm was as bad as he remembered them to be from those years in the desert. Strong winds blew grit and detritus at speeds that would abrade anything in their path. His bare hands screamed in agony as the skin was battered and torn by thousands of tiny granules. The leeward side of the first building became a sanctuary where the sand only lightly swirled about, instead settling onto any surface. It seemed drawn to their moistened eyes, clinging to them with a persistence that was almost supernatural. Filling their lungs, they darted from one shelter to the next, painstakingly making their way forward. By the time they reached the sandblasted steel towers of the United Nations headquarters, Alec's legs felt weak, and every step was effort. His lungs and eyes burned from the onslaught. He could hardly see through his own tears, and was taken by surprise when an eclectic group of soldiers bearing an assortment of weapons barred his way.

"Stand down, soldier," Fred ordered as he placed a calming hand on Alec's shoulder. "They're on our side."

Frederick and M'lanth unwrapped their faces, revealing themselves to the soldiers standing guard. Both were instantly recognized, but were still relieved of their weapons.

As the guards took Alec's dagger, Veleda leaned close and said, "Don't reveal your face until we have some space from the guards."

They were led up the stairs to the entrance and ushered inside the main hall. In the waking world, this space held a museum with testaments of disarmament, de-escalation, and aid to the weary of the world. Here, it was filled with exhibits of frightening weapons formed by some twisted and diabolical subconscious. What had in one place celebrated the hope of global unity was twisted into an eternal nightmare of war and genocide in this realm.

There was more on display than visions of war, however. Amid the gallery of destruction were exhibits ranging from implements of medieval barbarism to sleek futuristic machines of untold malignance. Living oil paintings of fallen heroes and tragic victims moved in continuous loops; saluting, fighting, dying, and posing heroically as their clothes fluttered in an unfelt wind. Windows that had once been clear were now festooned with barbed wire running through the glass. Brick and mortar were warped with twisted sculptures of all the demons of mankind's history. The terrible ambiance of the hall of horrors served only to accentuate the suffering of the refugees who now sheltered here. Ushered into a room of their own, the group were welcomed by a fountain bubbling with fresh water, translucent blue drinking glasses, and a bowl of ice chips.

Frederick rinsed his mouth of grit by sipping directly from the stream, while the ladies chose to use the offered vessels. As they did so,

Alec unwrapped the shirt from his face and shook it out over a wastebasket positioned in a corner of the room. The sand that fell was a fine dust. Content that the shirt was clean; he had been pulling it back over his head when the door opened and several guards rushed in and leveled their spears at his chest.

"I'm sorry," Alec said slowly. "I didn't know changing was illegal here."

Interposing herself between her guardian and those who threatened him, Veleda stared down the Resistance soldiers. Hesitantly, they lowered their weapons.

"Sorry, m'lady," one trooper apologized. "But he looks just like—"

"He is," M'lanth said, her quiet voice echoing off the walls. "That's why we're here. Assembly must be called."

The soldiers stared, hesitating, until irritation crossed the shadow-knight's face and she commanded, "Now."

Then they were gone. M'lanth slammed the door in frustration.

"Easy," Frederick said.

"It is no wonder most of our generals went to The Scourge's side! Discipline is still lacking."

"The Scourge?" Alec asked, still shaken by the sudden face-off.

"The enemy," Veleda explained.

Replacing his jacket, Alec said quietly, "It sounds like you admire our foe, M'lanth."

"I respect him," she admitted, "and if it weren't for Lady Veleda, maybe I would still be serving him."

An uncomfortable silence hung in the air for a few seconds before Alec asked, "Why?"

"Because of your kind, the Crafters!" she snapped, displaying a savagery that made her cloak amorphous once more. "Our world is not our own, but instead dominated and controlled by those who treat us as mere figments of imagination. We live, love, and hate based upon *your* subconscious desires, and are left stranded by *your* separation from us. Your land's violence destroys us, your hate envelops us, and all the horrors of your world leach constantly into our own."

A tear traced a path down her cheek, but M'lanth was too angry to wipe it away. "Do you know how acutely you control us, how little freedom we have? The Scourge has won many of his soldiers by promising to punish the creators, but he has lost many through his indiscriminate methods."

The shadow-knight ceased her tirade and wiped away the tears that now ran freely from her eyes. Alec stepped forward, suddenly wanting to offer a moment of companionship, but unsure of how his attention would be received.

"Can you tell me what happened?" he asked softly.

Presenting her back to the Crafter, M'lanth leaned on the wall for support as she spoke, her voice raspy, "She was thirteen, and she idolized those who fought for her people's freedom. Skin color determined her future, but she still had hope that things would improve so that she could better the world for others like her." M'lanth's fist clenched. "She was an optimist—foolish, but she had hope. One night, she went out on her first date. I knew because I felt her daydreaming. It was nothing more than a dance at a local community center. It was supposed to be simple and fun. She was supposed to be home before curfew.

"She never got the chance. The same bastards she fought to rise above—who mocked her, spat on her, and kept trying to break her—were waiting. They caught her and dragged her out of sight." M'lanth inhaled a ragged breath. Her misty cloak swirled about her, blocking out all but her face. From the darkness, sounds of violence, abuse, and pain emerged. Shapes formed in the fog, turning Alec's stomach.

The shroud dissipated, becoming her cloak once more as the shadow-knight whispered, "She died of her injuries days later. She was frightened, ruined, and delirious. I spent her last hours making her passing easier, playing back all of her favorite fantasies, and in the end I was the only one to tell her she was loved."

When she looked up at Alec, her eyes were red. "You idiots tore her away from me! Your kind callously killed an angel. I was happy that she believed in her dreams, but so many of you damn us instead that I cannot count all those who've suffered under your kind's dark desires."

Holding out her hands, M'lanth revealed the tattoos of her arms. "My first act as a soldier of The Scourge was to find the doppelgängers of those who had killed my Crafter. I tortured them for weeks until their own Crafters broke under the strain. For each one I shattered, I marked myself; trying to ease my own pain. This symbol, courage," she gestured to one particular tattoo, "was placed on my skin to remind me of the bravery that she faced her world with. This mark, purity, was to celebrate how her killers' deaths cleansed that world; even if only a little."

The images danced on her skin, each one a yin and a yang, a blessing and a curse.

"To this day, I have no regrets, but I wonder what might have been if I had acted sooner…"

The door opened. A bent over old man with wispy white hair and a long beard stood on the other side of it, escorted by the first uniformed soldiers that Alec had seen. They looked like Macedonian hoplites, but their armor was more complete, including masks and fully armored legs.

"You wish to call Assembly?" The old man's voice was thin and high, as if he spoke with a tightly pulled reed jammed in his airways. He smoothed his long yellow robes as he spoke.

"Yes, Elder Sage." Veleda pushed her way to the front. "I bring us hope."

All eyes fell on Alec. Years of discipline took over, and he carefully hid his surprise.

"The Creator." The elder's voice sounded impressed, but deflated as he spoke. "Lad, summon something, build us a Ghost."

"I'm sorry, I haven't been able to yet," Alec admitted.

"I see. Come, child," the elder extended a frail hand towards Veleda. "Walk with me."

She took his hand, and her guardians fell into step behind her. The elder seemed about to complain, but before he could, Veleda said confidently, "What concerns me concerns them."

Nodding, the elder took the Seer's other hand in his own. He spoke softly now, "I respect you, and I know that you are trying to help, but you bring us merely a *shadow* of a Crafter, someone who is so trapped in eternal Banality that he can offer no possible hope. I do not disagree that he is the origin of our foe, but he is weak where we need him to be as strong as a god. Already, The Scourge pounds on our gates, and our resources are dwindling. If you had brought us the miracle we needed, I could offer praise, but we cannot waste resources training a broken man, and broken he is. You can see that in him. Look into his eyes and tell me truthfully he is whole."

"I..." Veleda stumbled, lost for words. "I want to..." She looked towards Alec, who stood stoically absorbing the words of the elder.

"I wish to believe as well, my child. But until he releases himself from Banality and accepts the reality of our world, even in part, he is just another soldier."

Pausing, the elder released Veleda's hands from his own, "For now, I will let you stay here. My hope is that he finds his abilities, but until he does, he is not the miracle we seek."

Without another word, the Sage left. Sighing, Veleda pinched the bridge of her nose as if to push away the stress. Steeling herself, she roused the others. "Let's take him up on his offer and stock up on our supplies. Perhaps some rest will do us well." The last words were punctuated with pointed looks at the two Crafters in her midst. Cursing in an unknown tongue, she walked through the crowd and back to the room they had been offered.

* * *

"Hey, Fred?" Alec whispered into the darkened room. "Are you okay?"

"I'm well enough. What is it?" he asked.

"Can you teach me how to summon?"

Sighing, Frederick sat up from the couch he had been resting on. "I can try, but I won't make any promises. Close your eyes and try and make something. Convince your mind that you *need* it rather than just want it."

Alec tried to think of something, but his mind drew a blank. He focused on his breathing and tried to convince himself he needed *something*, but nothing became even remotely clear to him.

Fred's demeanor evolved from mildly annoyed to frustrated as Alec progressed from quiet thought to loud grunting, trying to force himself to conjure something. When his patience had finally waned, the commander stood and put one hand on his friend's shoulder.

"Face it, Alec." Frederick sighed. "You're still too attached to Banality."

Gasping as if he had run a marathon, Alec pleaded with his friend. "How do I become detached? How do I break free?"

"You have to believe that this reality is the truth." Frederick said. "I have an idea. Why don't you take a walk and try to notice the fantastic about you? Let's see if that helps your brain at all."

Nodding, Alec turned to leave, but a whistle from Fred stopped him. "Do yourself a favor and wear a disguise. You come off a little too obviously a Creator."

Ripping a blanket from the couch, Alec covered his face as he stepped into the main hall. Ignoring the sights, he jogged up stairs, across hallways, and down ramps. He kept moving faster and faster. Wanting to wear out his body and exorcise himself of his failures, he picked up his pace to a sprint; but no matter how fast or how far he ran; he still felt them chasing him.

He felt Kiso dying under his hands. He remembered Sylvain saying he was fine before his eyes glassed over and his voice fell flat. He smelled Frederick's charred flesh, a scent that lingered even after the treatments. He saw Frederick in the hospital, just after he had been sent home to live in a permanent stupor.

Only once he could barely stand did he bother to survey his surroundings.

It was fantastic, mystical, and would have caused anyone else to stare in wonder. He wished his brain would simply accept that a Tasmanian devil dressed in old-timey preachers' garb, a top hat, and a pair of six shooters was standing next to him in the hallway. An oil painting of two lovers staring hand-in-hand into an eternal sunset and aging from young women to old ladies before becoming youths again was simply there. A chimera of wolf and child groaning happily while a skeleton scratched its belly was perfectly normal.

It was a fact, simple as that.

It was a fact that he was in a strange land.

It was a fact that the shadows of the other world danced about before him, heading towards the exit and symbolizing closing time.

It was a fact that the pill rattled in his pocket, reminding him of its ever-constant presence.

It was a fact that he was in another realm, fighting for no reason of his own, other than he had been bored with his life.

It was a fact that he had left his blade behind upon the request of the elder.

It was a fact that people were screaming as armored soldiers began pouring into the hall, their uniforms and gear emblazoned with an image of a bloodied whip with multiple tails covered with razor blades.

It was The Scourge.

They had broken through.

CHAPTER 6

Alec ducked into a service hallway and slammed the door behind him as he cursed. He was without his blade, isolated, and his was a face worth selling out for.

"Great," he whispered to himself. "I have to get back to Veleda so I can protect her again."

The problem was, he had not paid attention to the route that had brought him here in his frantic flight.

He needed to find an escape, and now.

The first door that opened revealed a glass window laced and secured with razor wire. It wasn't going to break with simple persuasion alone.

A clanking noise caught his attention, and Alec looked into the hall to see the elder's guards moving towards him. Stepping back, he made room for them to pass, only for the soldiers to stop and level their spears at him.

"Crafter," the leader of the gang said, "come with us, for your protection."

Shrugging, Alec let himself be led about the winding corridors full of twists and turns until he found himself in the office of the yellow-robed elder.

"I take it you know that your building is under attack?" Alec asked casually.

The sage shot the warrior an annoyed look.

"We have begun evacuations," he hissed. "It would have been foolish for us to expect the unbound king to leave us alone. Fortunately, with you here, we have some room to bargain for better odds."

Alec didn't have to look back to know that the guards' weapons were still leveled against him. Narrowing his eyes, the guardian glared at the elder with unadulterated hatred as he was forced further into the room and surrounded by a ring of blades and armor. Tightening his core, he flexed his knees and relaxed his arms as he prepared himself for battle.

"This is a sick joke, *Elder*." Alec made the last word sound of a curse. "You are playing games, but you know my touch is far more permanent than others'. Arm me and let me help with the evacuations, I'm useless standing here."

The sage returned Alec's mockery. "Quite the contrary, *Crafter*. Your presence here will guarantee that the leadership of our army will continue to exist."

"I wasn't aware my ass was so valuable," Alec smiled.

"You have no idea of your own worth," the elder chuckled, straightening his yellow robes as he stood from behind his desk. "You think I can negotiate with you as my bargaining chip just because you are a creator? That just proves how ignorant your companions keep you."

"I've had hints that there is more to me than meets the eye," Alec replied dryly, examining the weapons surrounding him. His index finger forced aside a threatening spear that was too close to his face for comfort. "It matters little to me. I am here as a guardian for Veleda, noth—"

"That is precisely why you should be concerned," snapped the sage. "Don't think you are here by chance; she sought you out."

"Then I'm flattered."

"You should be scared." The last word was hissed. "I wonder; if you knew why you are so important, would you have stayed in Banality instead of coming here?"

Alec shrugged in reply. "Doesn't matter. I'm here now."

"Have you no sense of self-preservation, either?" the elder said incredulously.

"In Banality, I have been nothing but a shell wandering aimlessly in a haze. Banality was just that, banal. I was eking out a living, moving automatically through a monotonous routine. At least here I serve a purpose." Alec's eyes searched the room for an exit as he spoke.

"Even if that purpose is to sell you off?"

"Pot calling the kettle black, I see," Alec smirked.

"Without my leadership, the rebellion will fall."

"It's precisely because of sell-outs like you that the Resistance should fail," Alec snapped. "You don't have plans to benefit the innocent, only yourself. I've seen your kind too often to ignore the signs."

Growling, the elder stepped through the ring of spears so that he was almost close enough to touch.

"You have no understanding of the situa—"

Alec roared his interruption. "You're a coward who profits from the hordes you command! You've never once stained your hands with a day of work, yet they are covered in blood and bullshit!"

The two stared icily at one another. The sage stepped forward, refusing to be intimidated by Alec's cold glare, and the guardian sprang his trap. There had been no way to escape the circle of spears that surrounded him until the elder had forced open the ring by coming closer.

Leaping forward, Alec drove his knee into the sage's chest, bowling the wizened one over as he charged out of the ring of spear tips. As soon as he had cleared the ring, his escape seemed futile; the doorway was blocked; and there was no exit beyond the twisted window and its barbed wire infused glass.

A trio of guards lunged at Alec, stabbing at him with their spears. He avoided the first two, but the third one cut deep into his side, tearing both cloth and flesh before grating against bone. The spear pinned his jacket against the wall, trapping him. Alec felt the blow, but the pain was numbed by the adrenaline coursing through his body.

Sliding his right arm free of his jacket, Alec clubbed an attacker in the head with a closed fist, knocking the metallic helmet from his foe as the soldier charged forward. The soldier slammed into Alec and pinned his left arm against the wall, preventing him from pulling that one free of the jacket. The window behind him absorbed much of the impact, and cracked loudly behind him.

"Don't think you can hip-check a Habs fan and expect to survive," Alec snarled as he grabbed the guard's ornamental cape to pull him over, then delivered a quick blow from his knee to knock the man out cold.

"He's worth more alive!" shouted the elder. Two more guards dropped their weapons and threw themselves towards Alec, their impacts once more slamming him against the glass. The spreading of the cracks along the window was audible.

Alec threw an elbow into one of the attackers, but another two took his place.

"Is that all you've got?" he roared as he was once more smashed into the window, the razor wire tearing into his flesh over and over. The windowpane had finally had enough, and gave way in a shower of shattered glass that rained over the struggling warriors. As the throng pulled him to the ground, Alec freed his other arm from his coat.

Grabbing the flailing arm of an attacker, he jerked it out of the shoulder joint, wrenched the wrist, and pulled himself back to his feet, throwing his screaming victim to the ground. His victory was short-lived; the remaining guards tackled him, once more pushing him against the barbed wire that remained entangled in the shattered window frame. Unable to take the strain, the wires snapped one by one; barbs flailing about like angry scorpion tails, and Alec spilled out of the elevated window, along with most of the guards. They landed on a pillar of sand that had collected against the side of the building. It collapsed under the sudden weight, sending the mass of bodies upon it sliding down to the street below. Crushed stone, sandy grit, and shards of glass drove themselves into his flesh as he came to a stop. Stars swam before his eyes, and his ears filled with the roar of the sandstorm. He clutched the wound in his side, blood seeping between his fingers where the guard's spear had run him through.

There was no movement from the bodies that had come to a stop around him, and high above were the struggling shapes of the guards who were still ensnared in the wire. One of them gagged as a strand of it tightened around his neck. Blood oozed around his collar where the barbs dug in, and his fingers were flayed from struggling to loosen the makeshift noose. Within moments, his protestations came to a halt, and he hung swaying serenely in the breeze.

Over the wind, Alec could hear cries of pain, roars of hate, and screams of fear, mixed with the clash of weapons.

The clattering of hooves on the street undercut the cacophony of suffering. From within the swirling sandstorm, a knight charged forth on a red steed. Though the sand had scoured it, the emblem of a whip stood out on his shield. The head of the ship's spar in his hand was obscured by sand, as if the grains were adhering to a coating of blood. Then he was gone, lost again in the swirling clouds.

Swirling grit stung Alec's flesh, clogged his nose, and blurred his vision. He tore away an ornamental cape from one of the nearby corpses of the guards who had fallen with him, wrapping it around his face before he collected his bearings. He made his way towards Central Park, dashing off into the storm.

As he moved on, it grew worse. The winds accelerated until the friction of the blowing sand against his body felt as if it would burn him, even through his protective garments. The static charge in the air released itself through arcs of lightning that struck many armored warriors, and fighting spilled from the building into the streets. The bodies of warriors and civilians alike were strewn across the paths, some already disappearing under the blowing sands. The chaos made it impossible for Alec to maintain his sense of direction. He ran until his lungs ached and his knees trembled, but the park failed to appear. One hand still held his side; the flow of blood staunched more by the accumulating sand than his feeble attempt to slow it himself.

And he had lost his way.

He could barely see as he stumbled through the storm, and his lack of vision caused him to tumble halfway down a set of concrete stairs that took him out of the rushing winds. He landed on a pile of sand that would have been much higher if it hadn't been shoveled away recently.

Violent vibrations approached from one direction, and then suddenly faded away in the other. Alec knew something big and fast had just thundered by, and on closer inspection realized he had found the subway system, which hopefully meant he was in ally territory.

Collecting himself, Alec removed the cape from his head and balled it up before shoving it into the wound on his side. He knew he was risking an infection, but hoped the dream dust wasn't septic. At least it helped to stem the bleeding.

Holding the cape tightly to his side with his elbow, he limped the rest of the way down the stairs, coming to an iron gate where he would have expected a turnstile. Leaning against it, Alec wondered how he was going to make his way inside. The answer came as the gate fell open, causing him to land onto chilled concrete. He
lay there, letting the coolness soothe his face and relieved to finally be out of the rushing wind and away from the raging battle. Just as a sigh of contentment was about to pass his lips, a boot stomped down on his wounded flank.

"If you resist, you die," someone snarled.

"I'm too damn tired to fight back, so I guess I'll live." Alec groaned, rolling over to hide his injury from the next impact only to hear a sudden intake of breath.

"Let me guess, I look like '*him*', whoever '*he*' is," Alec moaned dryly.

"Yes." The creature who had kicked him was an amalgamation of a man and a rhinoceros, and covered in a host of brass plates, gears, and steam-based piston technology. It snorted, then rumbled, "Lady Veleda said to keep an eye out for you."

The hope and excitement in Alec's voice at the mention of her was impossible to hide. "She's safe?"

"Yes. She came to us; she and her family have always supported the less fortunate of the rebellion," the beast explained, holding out a hand.

Taking the offered hand, Alec grunted as he was pulled to his feet. "Good to know."

"C'mon," the beast said, supporting the wounded creator. "They're waiting for you at the park."

CHAPTER 7

It was the weirdest train he had ever ridden, because there was really no train at all. Encouraging his companion, the rhino walked to the edge of the platform and steadied Alec by bracing his neck.

"Just a precaution," it grumbled. "The first jolt is always the worst."

Stepping over the rail, the mechanized beast floated upward, hoisting Alec against its metal chest. As soon as it lifted its other foot free of the platform, the pair went thundering through the tunnels, levitated by some unseen force. They passed other platforms along the way, but saw few other travelers.

"Where is everybody?" Alec enquired.

"Evacuating," the rhino answered. "The upper class thought the island could be guarded, but few—if any—of the common folk thought the same."

"What is Lady Veleda's position, then?"

"Upper middle-class."

"That makes sense, I guess." Alec shrugged as best he could as they rounded the bend and the rhino leapt onto a rather crowded platform. With simultaneous cries of concern, both Veleda and Frederick ran to their wounded companion.

Alec's former CO inspected the wound in his side.

"How much blood have you lost? Is there any poison in the wound? How long have you been injured for?" he asked rapidly.

"Where were you? What happened?" Veleda asked.

"One at a time," Alec coughed. A medical kit arrived, and Fred began to dress the wound. As he did, Alec brought everyone up to speed with a quick recap.

"I see you three made it out relatively unscathed," he remarked when he had finished. "I'm glad."

"It helps if you listen to my instructions—" Frederick began, but Alec cut him off as M'lanth helped him to his feet.

"Check for all viable entrance and exit routes, have a backup, and never go into a room if there isn't an alternate escape available," he parroted the words he had heard from Frederick countless times as he surveyed the crowds of refugees.

"That's a lot of people," Alec noted. "Where are they all going? I don't think the glen will hold them all."

"It won't," Veleda admitted. "But it will choose some. They wait in hope, like those on a sinking ship awaiting a chance to sit on a lifeboat."

"And us?"

"Guaranteed passage." She sighed guiltily. "The glen will protect the rest of them for as long as it can, but there is little hope unless The Scourge can be stopped."

"And how do we do that?" Alec wondered. "The upper echelons seem more concerned with protecting their own asses than those of the people, and I haven't seen any real Resistance army."

"I...have a plan or two." Veleda said hesitantly. When she didn't continue, Alec didn't press the issue.

"The sooner we get going, the sooner we might have a solution," M'lanth reminded them all.

They followed the shadow-knight as she parted the crowds. Apparent guilt persuaded Veleda to keep her head bowed, and Frederick mouthed promises and apoloties to those he passed, but everyone in the crowd ignored the others as soon as they set eyes upon Alec's face. He heard them muttering:

"It's him!

It must be his Creator!

How did they capture him?"

Hands reached out as people begged them for salvation. Children cried, and adults either openly wept or remained stone-faced as the four reached the top of the sand-shrouded stairs.

The journey to the glen was mercifully short, and the standstorm hid the sounds of despair and desperation they left behind. Falling to his knees in the soft grass of the glen the moment they arrived, Alec closed his eyes and swallowed against the pain.

"Where to now?" he winced.

"We need supplies to treat him," Frederick said to the others, "unless we want to wait two weeks for him to heal. He's still burdened by flesh and blood, unlike the rest of us."

Veleda's sighed in frustration. "We have less than two days before the Resistance are found and overrun." She hesitated, as if she wanted to add some other detail. Biting her lower lip, she looked at Frederick. "We need him in prime condition, if possible."

"Stenshuvud has what I need," the commander said quietly. "But we must be quiet; the fortress is occupied by our enemy, and the Giddastuan giant is easily upset."

"The what?" Alec asked, but Fred motioned for him to wait.

"So be it," Veleda said. As she closed her eyes, the sky shifted from the deep amber of the setting sun to the black pitch of a moonless night. Gone was the hissing of the wind, replaced with a billowing roar that drew all eyes to a grand castle only a short walk away. The structure's ramparts climbed high into the heavens, its white marble walls gleaming brightly in the darkness. A garrison of soldiers screamed in horror as they fought valiantly against a giant creature that ignored the hail of arrows, stones, and fire that they hurled at it. It reached over the walls with ease, scooping a dozen troops, armor and all, into its enormous maw.

"So much for needing to be quiet," Frederick said softly, awe filling his tone. Grabbing his spear, he motioned to M'lanth, who was already cloaked in misty shadows. The two hurried off into the surrounding woods.

Closing his eyes, Alec fell into a fitful slumber.

*   *   *

"You had many chances to deliver. My patience has worn thin." Whoever spoke sounded like they were used to being the sole voice of authority. "You could have simply left him for my men to capture if you didn't have the heart to deliver him yourself."

Alec's stomach knotted as he cracked his eyes open. Veleda was standing by the pool in the glen, speaking to water that had fountained upwards and taken the shape of an armored figure.

"His escape was not my doing. Rest assured, you shall have him presented to you by next sundown, as promised," Veleda hissed through clenched teeth.

The fountain water wavered and dissipated, sinking once more into the placid pool. With a sigh of regret, the Seer looked to where Alec had been lying prone only to see him standing to her left. Gone from his face was any sense of compassion, gone was any sense of mercy, any warmth. He had an almost bored expression, but his anger was apparent.

"Which of us do you plan to betray?" His voice was flat and emotionless as he requested the facts. "And to whom are you planning to sell them?" His hands balled into fists, knuckles white from the strain. "Is it me? Is that why you brought me here?"

"This is not what you think," she said.

"Oh really?" Alec advanced, ignoring the rustling of the glen as it prepared to defend its friend. "Aren't you planning to sell me off?"

"Only as a last resort."

"To The Scourge?"

"Yes." Veleda admitted, the word escaping her blackened lips in a sigh.

"So they can do what? Kill a creator? Make my death a show of power?" His voice began to rise as fury filled him.

"No, he wants to kill *his* creator!"

"'His creator...'" Alec repeated the words as the weight of them fell upon him. He was the creator of the Scourge
? The enemy these people fought against was his own doppelgänger? Th
at was why the people of this world looked upon him with such awe and fear. "Why? I thought a doppelgänger's mind only warped when its Creator died."

"He has already been broken from you." Veleda's back pressed against a tree, stopping the slow retreat she had been making as Alec spoke. Raising her arms in front of her face, she turned her head and closed her eyes as if anticipating blows of rage.

"How is that possible?" Alec whispered through clenched teeth.

"You stopped dreaming."

The weight of the pill dragged at Alec's side. He paused his advance, and she hurried to explain.

"He's holding my family hostage unless I can deliver you by tomorrow night. If I don't, he's going to kill them. I had hope that your banality would fade enough for you to challenge him. You could save my blood, and unseat him entirely, but only if your mind allows the fantastic within—"

"You think I'm a lost cause?"

Veleda cast her eyes to the ground. "Yes," she answered. "I fear you are. You cannot face him. You built him when you were at your darkest."

"So why does he want to kill me?"

"Those like your friend's doppelgänger, who are close to their creators, have capabilities beyond the rest of us." Realizing that he was not going to strike her, she stood straighter. "There is a myth that if a doppelgänger touches their creator, they will be absorbed and returned to their host's mind. That is not what he wants. The Scourge has researched extensively, consulting many sources, and he is certain that if you die in his presence he can absorb *your* soul instead. If he does this, he believes he will ascend to something greater than Ccreator or doppelgänger."

"How do you know this?" Alec asked.

"He forced me to read his mind, to see if you still existed and if you would be a threat."

"Am I?" Her guardian laughed sarcastically. "You are a Seer, you pulled me into your land. Why don't you look into the darkest depths of my soul and find out for yourself what I am?"

Alec spread his arms and leaned forward to offer himself to her. Hesitantly, she reached out one hand and touched two fingers to his eyes, placing another two about his lips. They exhaled as one, and the she recoiled in shock.

"Are you happy with what you have seen?" Alec asked, "Do you see the darkness within?"

"There is not just darkness within you." Veleda clutched at her heart. "I know if that was true, I'd be dead already."

"I am a killer," he confessed as he stepped closer to her, waiting for her to acknowledge his sins. "The darkness is mine to bear. I have repressed it with the restraints of civilized etiquette, but darkness is all I am, and it is my weapon, the dragon within me. Kindness and civility is just my mask."

"You have darkness inside of you," Veleda said quietly. Her hands reached out until her fingers glided over his palms. "But that's not all." She brought Alec's hands up in front of his chest. "These hands have also healed, and this heart," one hand now rested on her guardian's breast, "beats for those you've saved; and those who've saved you. You suggest you kill without regret; but while that's true, you still bear the scars of your actions."

"Even if that's the case, is there enough light to block out the dark?"

"There's enough to find the path," Veleda smiled, "and by simply finding the path, you are moving forward."

Stepping away, Alec's hand went to the pill bottle in his pocket. "What if I want to pretend this is a dream? What would you do then, now that you have seen something else in me?"

She sighed and turned away. "If it's not too late, I would let you go. If you still see the shadows of the other world, you can return."

"Is there still a chance I can challenge The Scourge?"

"Only if you allow yourself to dream. There is still hope to sever yourself from Banality."

Removing the phial from his pocket, Alec held it up for Veleda to see. "You've read my mind, what is this?"

Her answer was hesitant, nervous. "A stabilizer. You were issued it after the assault."

"It was attempted murder, don't sugar-coat it," he spat. "This is how they *'helped'* me, and this is how they cursed your land. With this, I can hardly feel. With this, I cannot dream. I haven't taken it for several days, yet I don't feel different. Is dreaming lost to me?"

The Seer's tone was soft. "Allowing yourself to love, and to remember, can set you free."

"How can I remember to dream?" he pried.

"Where we are going next may help," she said.

"And where's that?"

"The Library of Dreams," Veleda smiled softly. "Alexandria."

CHAPTER 8

"It survived after all." Alec stared in wonder at the building before him. "Here, in the dreamscape."

It was a great building of columns and arches, ringed by a modern circle of steel and glass, all built around a central towering ziggurat.

"What should I expect to find? What am I looking for?" Alec wondered aloud.

"Yourself," M'lanth answered. "Every dream ever had by a creator is held within."

Dipping into the sand they stood upon with his hand, Alec stared in disbelief. "How? The dreamsands underneath us alone would fill several floors."

"Unlike the sands, the library only holds the records of creators," the shadow-knight said flatly. "The rest of us serve it, as is our *'duty'*." She sneered the last word with naked hostility.

"We are built upon each other," Veleda said to M'lanth, who merely sucked her teeth in protest.

"We'd best hurry," the Seer continued. "Time is of the essence." She strode forth, urging the others to follow as she approached the grand steps. Towering pillars, each one bearing styles of disparate cultures and periods, supported the roof. Jogging to keep up, Alec placed his foot upon the first step and paused when neither M'lanth nor Frederick followed.

The shadow-knight turned her back and scanned for threats. "My place is best served guarding the gates," she said.

Frederick also turned away, refusing to look his friend in the eyes. "I dare not enter. There are rumors about that place; about those who refused to leave because they lost themselves. I don't think I could resist the urge to follow in kind. I am already so joined to this world that a single glance will lose me forever, be it at my dream or someone else's."

"A valid fear," M'lanth agreed.

"I'm sorry," Frederick said softly, his eyes downcast.

Alec hesitated, unsure whether or not he should offer comfort to his friend. Indecision rooted him in place for a few moments, but squaring his shoulders, he marched up the steps and grabbed the ornately carved door, holding it open for Veleda and following her inside.

It was much larger within than without. Countless rows of shelves stretched as far as the eye could see, towering to bewildering heights. Far above, great stained-glass windows depicting mythical beasts let in dazzling displays of colored light that pranced across the infinite shelves. The light danced through the space as each image transformed into something new and equally bizarre.

All this paled in comparison to the majestic crystalline beasts that stood even higher than the impossibly tall shelves. Egg-shaped bodies, pearlescent as opal, balanced on four multi-jointed legs. Some of the creatures stood patiently in the aisles, while others moved with purpose; roaming amongst the rows of books and organizing the infinite numbers of scrolls and tomes and tablets, or catching grains of floating dreamdust in their silken tentacles to be twisted into fine strands of fiber. These fibers were either woven before becoming a completed book, or were added to the pages of an existing volume. Seemingly weightless, the crystalline creatures moved silently, their bodies casting reflections in the polished granite floors that looked like stars dancing under their feet.

"What am I looking for?" Alec asked Veleda in hushed tones, afraid that too loud a sound would attract a giant's attention.

"Old dreams," Veleda whispered, "from before your ability to craft was lost. By finding them, maybe you will remember how you once crafted."

Facing the giants, the seer spread her arms and spoke in a voice not much louder than before. "Honored Librarians, I—Veleda of Neviah—request permission to view the stories of Crafter Alec LeGuerrier."

One of the waiting behemoths sank swiftly to the floor as its long tendrils flattened into a platform, and taking Alec's hands in hers, Veleda stepped onto the makeshift dais.

The giant creature moved impossibly fast. One moment, they stood at the entrance, and then there was a burst of colors, and a sudden pressure forced them against its satin appendages. When the pressure ceased, they were deep inside the library—so far in that Alec saw neither entrance nor exit, just endless rows of bookshelves.

"Look," Veleda pointed, "it's you."

Alec stared at the volumes stacked on the shelves before him. He had once upon a time written romances filled with desires, charged bravely across lands in search of conquest, and defeated countless foes, and it was all there for him to live again and again in written word.

"Careful," Veleda warned. "Many have lost themselves in their past and failed to write their final stories."

Reaching over to a shelf tentatively, he pulled down a small children's book titled *'I Can Fly'*. Trembling fingers spread the pages, and there he was, flying through oil paintings and pastel sketches. He felt the wind in his face, the softness of his childhood pajamas, and heard his own child-like laughter as he spun in loops and spirals.

He slammed the book closed and collapsed to his knees, his head shaking from side to side as tears ran like rivers down his cheeks.

"I remember. I was five," he whispered. "Mom and Dad let me stay up late to watch *Superman*, and I fell asleep on Dad's chest."

Like a thirsty man on the edge of death who had spied a glass of water, he grabbed another book.

He was a knight in shining armor who rode a dragon. On one arm, he wore a shield, while the other wielded a gargantuan lance. He was fighting for his kingdom, and his betrothed, Minné, who awaited rescue; for which she would reciprocate with…

He was on a breakaway. Although his skates slipped over the ice and his stick corrected the puck, all he could hear was the crowd chanting his name. If he made the goal, it would be the overtime win that earned he and his team the Stanley Cup…

"Careful, Alec," Veleda warned. "You risk losing yourself."

He, Sylvain, and Kosi had known each other since college, and had enlisted together for various reasons. Tomorrow they were heading to basic, but for that night,

they were three Musketeers, the most elite of his Majesty's guards. They fought valiantly against Cardinal Richelieu's men with nobility, honor, and panache. Crying out victoriously, Frederick swung himself over the gap between the floating airships. With a grunt, Kosi knocked aside the pistol that had been aimed at Alec's heart while Sylvain ran their foe through with his rapier. The four had to act fast, because once the enemy airship was over France, it was going to drop chemicals that would make the ground infertile, forcing the French people into starvation…

"Alec…" Veleda's voice was distant as he feverishly grabbed another tome.

Bullets flew through the sky, sounding like angry hornets as they passed by his head. Frederick was calling to him, but Alec didn't pay heed. He was too concerned with trying to stop the bleeding from Kosi's chest to keep his friend alive.

"Câlice, Alec. Find some cover."

"I got this! I can save him!" Alec knew as a medic that it was best to stay emotionally detached, to function like a machine, but he couldn't block out his feelings. Kosi wasn't just a friend; he was a brother. Their relationship had been forged over their entire lives and tempered in the heat of combat.

"They're shooting at you!" the Lieutenant screamed, but his words barely registered over the ringing in Alec's ears.

"They haven't hit me yet! Hold on, I'm clamping the artery—"

Another buzz, and a bullet missed Alec and plunged directly into Kosi's head, spraying his brains all over the ground. Enraged, Alec grabbed his rifle and fired at the approaching enemy. Bodies fell as he panned from one target to the next, toppling over as bullets slammed into them. This mission was supposed to be a simple task; the convoy was on their way to reinforce a forward operations outpost. Everything was routine, and their route through the village was supposedly safe. Everything had been going as planned until the lead and rear vehicles had simultaneously exploded.

Someone charged from an alley, covered in white robes with a knife in hand. Sylvain shot him in the legs, and the would-be martyr fell screaming to the sand-choked alleyway.

"I'm marking our position!" Frederick called as he popped a smoke grenade. *"Air support is inbound."*

His own weapon empty, Alec picked up Kosi's rifle. He paused to close his friend's eyes and break his I-Disk in half, whispering well wishes to his battle brother's soul…

"Alec, you must stop." Whose voice was that? Was it Kosi? Frederick? Sylvain?

Alec was walking home from the bar, having tried to drown out the memories. He had failed. Sylvain was dead by his own hand. His friend had never been able to leave behind the horrors they had shared; and two days ago he had left his wife and child at home, jumped in his car, and driven away. They had identified his body that morning. He had been found sitting in his car down a country road surrounded by empty bottles of booze, an empty vial of sleeping pills resting on the dash. When Alec told Frederick as his old CO lay in a drug induced stupor, a tear had rolled down Frederick's face. After paying his respects, Alec wandered alone. He could not talk to his father, who hadn't ever served, he had no girlfriend to console him, and Veteran Affairs had issued him a new doctor he didn't feel like he could talk to. The rest of the local legion had already called it a night as they had jobs to go to in the morning.

Someone stepped out of the alley, knife in hand. He heard a voice demanding money, shouting, but Alec was back in the sands among shitty mud shacks. All he saw was the charging youth in white robes, only this time Sylvain wasn't there to put him down. Alec snapped the boy's elbow, dislocated his shoulder, broke his knee, and finally smashed his face into a brick wall. The judge later ruled it excessive force and attempted manslaughter, but he sympathized with the troubled soldier and was lenient. He issued the minimum sentence and ordered him to take the medication that would ease his emotions, but rob him of his dreams...

Weeping, Alec shut the book and threw it as far from him as he could before collapsing to the smooth stone floor. He did not notice the Librarian plucking it from the air with a slender tendril to replace it on the shelf in its proper order.

Veleda knelt and gathered him into her arms, stoically cradling her guardian like a maternal effigy as he wept like a child in her embrace. He drifted off to sleep, and for the first time in ages he dreamed. He said goodbye to his fallen comrades, and when he awoke again, he was born anew.

CHAPTER 9

Frederick and M'lanth still waited outside, nervously facing the night. The sun had risen, climbed across the sky, and set again. Frederick himself had gone and returned, abandoning his doppelgänger for some time before returning to find nothing had changed. The sounds of footsteps behind them caused M'lanth to turn, her blades drawn. Frederick gripped his spear, holding it at the ready.

The knight that stood before them was adorned in living, pulsing armor. The emerald plate of it gloriously reflected the moonlight, shining with its own ethereal glow. After pausing a moment as if he was seeing the world anew, Alec hurried to take Frederick's cheeks in his palms and leaned forward to press a gentle kiss against his lips, a salty tear shared between them.

They parted from their intimate moment, and Alec pressed his forehead against his friend's as he wept unashamedly.

"I was told that if I love, and let myself be loved, I could dream again. I was told that dreaming could let me feel, and I do. I feel hope for the future, hope for a cause, and hope for us." The Crafter laughed even as tears rolled down his cheeks. He fought to keep speaking through the emotions that ran shudders through his body like the tremors of an earthquake. So used to feeling nothing, he was overcome by how acute everything had become under the influence of the heart.

"I only wish I'd known you felt the way you do about me a few months ago," Alec whispered, "then maybe my life—*our lives*—would be different."

Fighting back his own tears, Frederick asked, "How? I'm trapped in a useless shell, and you aren't even in my reality anymore."

"We'll find a way. We found each other here," Alec promised, kissing Frederick again and smiling with joy for the first time in years. "But first, I'm going to right my wrongs, so I need you to wait for me for one more night."

"Let me come with you!" Frederick pleaded, his hands grasping the shoulders of the man he loved.

"No, I can't. If anyone other than Veleda and I enter the grounds, they will be executed on the spot. Find a safe place, and we'll let you know once we've succeeded."

Frederick seemed about to protest, but then the commander bit his lip and turned his head. Saying nothing, Alec drew him into one more embrace before he began walking purposefully towards the wandering glen that awaited them beyond the sands surrounding the library.

Left alone, the commander raised his hand in salute as he watched the others walk out of sight. It was too painful to say goodbye, as everyone knew it may be their last.

Soon, the trees of the wandering glen replaced the once sand-swallowed lands.

*   *   *

They walked out of the glen, and Alec stopped, shaking his head in disbelief. "Casa Loma? Really?" What had been a palace of luxurious opulence adorned with gothic architecture in his former reality had become a fearsome and towering citadel in this one.

Armed guards stood in abundance along buttresses teeming with artillery. A moat filled with acidic sludge was stirred by long, ropey worms that surged into a frenzy of motion to feast on a bird that had flown too close to it The fountain was now a deep fenced-off reservoir. High overhead, an airship was docked at a spire, a painting of a whip emblazed upon its side so that all who saw the grand balloon knew whom to fear.

"I see my other self is not one for subtlety," Alec said with a hint of admiration. "So, do we waltz through the front door; or is there a way we can sneak inside?" he asked, looking back towards the Seer. He paused as M'lanth drew a bloodied finger across Veleda's face, hiding her tattoos with fresh crimson.

"The servants' entrance is your best chance," the shadow-knight said. "It is the least guarded, but most taxing point of entry.

"The Scourge forces all of his arrested servants to pass through a tunnel that is too short to stand upright in, making them to crawl for hundreds of feet, past frescoes of his greatness. The only way to graduate from there is by winning favour, and the egress route is even lower in height." M'lanth's tone was matter-of-fact now. "I am honored to have fought by your side, creator. Come what may, you have earned my respect."

She stepped back to admire her work. Veleda blinked, making sure no blood ran into her eyes.

The grate of the servants' entrance was not hard to find. It was a heavy portcullis that one had to lift and slide underneath if they wished to pass. The whole contraption was recessed into a pit, and as they watched, three feeble laborers struggled with it together in order to head to their duties. Two brutish guards hurried the trio along with the sting of their whips, so distracted that they failed to notice the intruders' approach until it was too late to raise the alarm.

Dropping an unconscious soldier face-first into a puddle of mud, Alec hissed, "Let's go." He slid past the grateful trio of servants and bent to lift the gate, but Veleda stopped him.

"You don't have to do this," she said slowly. "There's still time for you to return, time for you to find Frederick and share your lives together."

Blurred images swayed across Alec's vision, the final faint ghosts of his past reality. To pass through this door was to seal his fate.

Reaching into his pocket, Alec withdrew the phial and held it before the Seer's eyes before hurling it as far as he could into the waters of the reservoir.

"I refuse to return to somewhere where I was dead inside," he said. "Besides, if I succeed, we will share our dreams. Are you coming?"

He waited as shadow-knight and Seer held forearms and tenderly kissed each other's cheeks. As they parted, M'lanth threw her robe over Veleda's shoulders.

"You look like the soldiers I left behind," the dark one said, handing the Seer the dagger that Alec had claimed as his own when he had first crossed over. "If you get close enough, do not hesitate."

"I won't." Veleda promised.

"Guardian," M'lanth whispered, "keep my Lady safe."

He smiled and nodded in affirmation before he forced open the heavy iron gate and followed Veleda inside.

CHAPTER 10

His armored fingers beat a heavy staccato rhythm against the arm of his throne. The polished steel of his gear was dented and scratched from many a brutal campaign, and the points of the fingers were so claw-like that each touch dug tiny gouges into the stone.

Watching nervously were his generals and council. They knew why their king was anxious, and they prayed he did not lash out recklessly. The Scourge's temper was well known—the victims of his fury were now little more than stains upon the marble floor of his throne room.

Pointing, he spoke, his voice carrying for all to hear, "If the Librarians don't acquiesce within the next five minutes, set fire to the books."

"Yesss, my Lord," a thin reptilian officer hissed as he bowed.

After rising from his seat of power, The Scourge paced back and forth across the floor. His ornate metallic armour bore decorations of his victories, which remained clearly visible despite the wear of countless battles. The plates were intricately linked, and despite their bulk, posed no hindrance to his movement. No cape nor lanyard hung free from it, and no ornamentation protruded from the carved plates themselves. It was armor designed for war—gilded, but baptized in blood.

Staring out of the throne room's grand window, which opened to a balcony, he dismissed most of his subordinates with a wave. Only his four bodyguards remained still. The protectors were dressed in plain versions of his armor—each suit bereft of the grandeur of his own—and stood in separate corners of the rectangular hall. Two slept where they stood, while the other two were alert.

Another figure entered, their heavy footfalls echoing around the vast space. Scars crossed his face, and blackened, charred flesh clung to his arms and hands. The sword he wore strapped on his back was more of a butcher's tool than a blade designed for combat.

"Report, Sylvain," The Scourge demanded, not having to look to know it was the doppelgänger who, like him, had lost his Crafter.

"The glen still protects those it embraces, but it won't for much longer, sir." The voice that replied was raspy and garbled as the doppelgänger fought to speak through the scars on his throat. Before his Crafter had left the dreamscape forever, the dream-form had endured manifestations of his creator's guilt, suffering constantly every time the human dreamed. "Permission to join the troops and finish the job?"

"Denied." The Scourge's response was light, almost cheerful. "I may have need of your talent for execution if a certain package hasn't arrived when the sun sets in a few short minutes."

Clothed in simple rags with their faces shielded and their vision occluded by strips of leather—so as not have their vile gazes sully the room—eight indentured servants carried in the Font of Focus; a tool of long-distance communication The Scourge had stolen as his own. Each bearer was bound at the neck with loops of untreated hide that had been tied together to form a yoke, and all were guided by the pull of a sole shadow-knight.

Walking slowly towards them as if he were enjoying a stroll, The Scourge laughed. "You know, Sylvain," the leader said lightly, "in hindsight, I should not have underestimated the love of family. You know of the deal I made with the Lady of Neviah?"

Grabbing one of the bound, The Scourge examined the young woman's features. He squeezed her face, forcing her lips outward in his powerful grip as he leaned down and kissed them softly. He searched for signs of welcoming or disgust, but when all he tasted was fear, he let her go and moved onto the next servant.

"I am aware." Sylvain watched with detached emotion as The Scourge inspected a young boy, tousling the lad's hair in passing.

"Then know that I'm sorry."

A hulk of a man quivered under his ruler's touch, and The Scourge moved on.

"Apparently," As The Scourge removed their blindfold, an elderly androgynous person stared calmly back at him. Pausing, his hand at the ready on his blade, The Scourge looked back at his friend. "I called you here for naught."

*　*　*

The blade was drawn so fast it barely had time to flash in the light before the king stabbed it into the suddenly empty cloth. As if ejected from the garment, Alec sank low and slid across the chamber with a bent knee and one hand on the polished floor before slowly coming to a controlled stop; the fading daylight glinting off of his emerald armor.

"Did you honestly think I wouldn't sense your presence?" The Scourge sounded insulted. "We were once one, you and I, and unlike you, I never forgot that."

Alec stood and brushed casually at his armor. "Maybe we were united once, but you are nothing like me anymore."

"I accept your compliment." The Scourge snapped his fingers, urging the shadow-knight to remove the remaining blindfolds from the slaves. He kept his eyes on Alec, confident that his orders would be carried out without question, but the shadow-knight turned on him. Her dagger flashed as she prepared to hurl it at his back, only for it to be knocked from her hand by the unnaturally fast slash of an enormous cleaver.

She had barely realized what happened when the burned and battered Sylvain collided with her. The shadow cloak's hood fell back, revealing Veleda's face, filled with surprise at the savagery of the attack. In moments, she was pinned to his body by his terrible strength, the heavy cleaver held just under her throat. Seeing that Sylvain had everything under control, the guards, who had barely had time to tense, relaxed.

Turning to the Seer, Alec's doppelgänger extended his hand. "Your family shall live, child; but for your offence, you shall not. Sylvain, keep her restrained. I'll deal with her once I'm done with my Crafter."

"You mean once *I'm* done with *you*," Alec sneered.

"You *are* me." The Scourge laughed brazenly. "You are the original who fully embraced Banality and forgot whimsy, casting me aside; yet I refused to die. Though I was once your shadow, I embraced what you had made me. I am the greatest parts of who you were, and in minutes, I will be grander than anything that has ever walked either this realm of Fancy *or* the realm of Banality."

Crafter and doppelgänger began to circle each other like beasts, each sizing up their foe, searching for a weakness, and waiting to see who would strike first. The emerald champion and ebony king moved slowly, their orbits drawing them closer to each other.

"You think yourself superior?" the doppelgänger laughed, "You are a hollow imitation of the man who forged me. I was molded after granite, yet my spies and soldiers tell me you are as brittle as gypsum."

"The men who faced me died; I highly doubt you should let the whispers of corpses guide your plans," Alec said with a wry smile.

The Scourge laughed bitterly again. "You are nothing more than a neophyte dreamer."

"I'm still a Crafter," his creator said. "I'm a threat to you, and you know that."

"You're still figuring out how to be a god, but I already *am* one," spat the king, snapping his fingers.

The fountain in the center of the chamber burbled as water shot into the air, and Frederick's beaten and bloody body became visible. His arms were tied to a yoke, and he rested on his knees, his battered lungs gasping for air as his voice wheezed, "He knows now. He is coming to get you. You will all pay…"

"Fred!" The pain in Alec's voice radiated throughout the throne room. Taken aback, Veleda clutched her chest.

Enraged, Alec swelled to his full height, rolled his shoulders back, cracked his neck, and then spoke in an icy whisper, "What did you do to him?"

"Ambush," his doppelgänger shrugged. "Frederick may be a decent fighter, but he's a healer first. He almost always holds back from the coup-de-grâce. It makes him easy to exploit, especially given he stayed behind to protect the library when he felt us coming."

Stretching as if staying combat-ready had left him tense, the doppelganger added, "Did you know he screams like a bitch?"

The Scourge knew his words would elicit a reaction, but he still seemed taken aback by his Crafter's savagery as it was unleashed. Growling like a feral dog, Alec swung, but it was a wild attack. Despite its speed, The Scourge easily blocked the punch and replied by driving his own clenched fist directly into Alec's chest. The blow was so strong that its impact flung the Crafter through the nearest wall in a cascade of broken stone. As he landed, Alec could see his shadowy twin striding towards him through the billowing dust of the collapsing masonry.

Gathering all of his strength, Alec leapt back through the crumbling wall, landing before the advancing Scourge with a crash, and cracking the marble floor under his verdant gauntlet. The green mask that he had moved to obscure his face shifted as he tracked his foe. With surprising speed, the king's armored shin caught Alec in the face, knocking him aside as the impact cracked his glittering helmet.

The Scourge stayed tight to his foe, his hands already grabbing and twisting Alec into a position that left him entirely at his doppelgänger's mercy. Without hesitation, The Scourge threw him upwards, smashing Alec into the ceiling. The stunned Creator fell, a kick to the chest throwing him across the length of the room before he hit the ground. Alec's head spun, and sirens rang in his ears. The emerald armor had cracked from the blows, and bits of it fell to the ground in a glittering rain as he struggled to his feet. He raised his arms to deflect the next attack, but was forced backwards, his boots digging into the solid stone as if it were as malleable as butter.

Finding himself beside the throne, Alec grabbed the great stone seat and ripped it free. Roaring in rage, he brought it down over his doppelgänger's shoulder; only to see it rendered to splinters as The Scourge drew and swung his blade in one fluid motion. The steel became a blur that crashed into Alec's chest plate, cracking his armor further and sending him sprawling onto his back.

"I was forged out of your hate and fury; from your fire and rage!"

The sword descended, but Alec rolled away, the blade slicing into the marble floor where he had been. He tried to rise, but a boot caught him in the chest and slammed him against the wall with a loud crunch. Fire burned in Alec's lungs as more of the broken armor fell away. His vision swam before him, and all he could see was the blur of the ebony-armored Scourge advancing upon him once more.

"Do not think yourself superior simply because you birthed me." The Scourge's sword slammed against Alec's armor again, sounding like a thunderclap upon impact. "You lack the imagination to even defend yourself, let alone defeat me."

A glowing shield blossomed like a flower over Alec's left arm, blocking the blow meant to break him. Forming a knife-hand with his right, the creator lunged.

His glowing fingers peeled back The Scourge's armor as if it were foil instead of plate, but he failed to wound his doppelgänger's flesh further as his opponent retreated with blinding speed.

"What I make, so shall I destroy," gasped the creator, who pulled himself from the wall and strode forward with renewed confidence.

Unafraid, The Scourge chuckled and threw a dagger from his belt. Rather than deflect it, Alec moved like lightning to avoid the projectile. He ran up one pillar and leapt to another, and then another, until he was mere meters away from his enemy. Lazily, his doppelganger punched the air with his blade raised, catching the swiftly moving Alec by surprise. So great was the counterattack that Alec's damaged armor shattered, disintegrating into a shower of emerald as he was slammed back against the column he had just leapt from. He slid to the ground in a heap of bruised and bloodied flesh.

"My spies were right!" roared the king. "You may be good against the feeble and uninitiated, but you can't even lay a hand on me."

Flailing onto his hands and knees, Alec tried to breathe, but his body failed to respond. An iron hand closed over his throat, lifted him, and slammed him against the broken stone column.

"No doppelgänger has ever killed their Crafter before. When I take your life, I will be the first of my kind to control the dreamscape." With every other word, Alec was slammed into the column. "I will be what you made me to be, a conqueror."

He wanted to respond, but Alec's head was spinning from the blows, and he could not even find the will or focus to spit at his foe in defiance. He fought through the fog in his mind long enough to mutter, "All I see is a big talking pile of—"

The pain as the blade fell upon one shoulder, cleaving it from Alec's body, was excruciating. Before the limb hit the ground, The Scourge spun and buried his blade into the opposite shoulder. At least the agony awoke Alec from the fog in his head.

Confident in his victory, The Scourge turned his back on his foe and walked away, arms spread as he cawed, "A shallow mold, at best."

Chuckling, the king cast his gaze upon the Seer. "You may have read my mind once, but I doubted you still could once we were apart. I knew you were aligned with the rebels, so if you had died during our little display in his reality, I would have shed no tears." Once more, The Scourge studied Alec's waxing face. "It was too easy to lure you in. All you needed was a reason to fight again, a cause. You felt lost, and I gave you a sense of duty. The three goons you killed were all for show. You were serving *me* all along."

Resting his head against the cold stone of the pillar, Alec tried to breathe and gather his strength. He felt the blood pouring from his severed shoulder, warmth flowing down one side of his body as blood pulsed out of him with every beat of his heart. All the while, his doppelgänger strutted about victoriously.

Desperate to go down fighting, Alec willed away the pain. The Scourge was right, he *couldn't* lay a hand on him, but he didn't need to. As his doppelgänger once more turned his back to Alec to gloat to the Seer, her guardian pulled the blade from his shoulder and gathered his legs beneath him. He leapt, falling upon The Scourge's back. Wrapping his one arm around his opponent's neck, the Crafter dug his fingers into the open wound that had been his other shoulder. Crimson life fluids poured from his body, leaking into the joints and gaps of his doppelganger's armor.

"What are you hoping to accomplish? Are you trying to drown me in your own blood?" The king laughed.

Grunting, Alec gouged his wound harder as he clung to his foe. Every beat of his heart sent more of his blood through the gaps, every struggle increased its flow. Bracing his legs, Alec straightened his back as if he was trying to choke his doppelgänger by yanking on his neck.

Still cackling, the king backed up and slammed Alec against the pillar. His resolve tightening even as his grip slackened, Alec hung on.

"Please," he whispered to himself. "Just one more minute."

"Just as stubborn as ever," The Scourge sighed, took a step forward, and prepared to ram his Crafter back into the standing stone. He stopped suddenly, realizing that something was wrong.

Something was very wrong.

The blood had run in rivulets down the king's back, seeping in and out of the joints in his armour, and had found a path that intercepted the blood flowing from his own wounds.

A channel had been built; a conduit of physical contact.

"NO!" he screamed, finally realizing what Alec had done. "NO!" He thrashed and fought, trying to throw his Crafter clear. His body began to burn, but even though his motions bucked his Crafter about, Alec would not release him.

"Sylvain, help me!" the king pleaded, and the charred one began to hurry to his side. As he did, Veleda, her eyes black with fury, caught Sylvain's legs. Enraged, the soldier turned to slap her, but found his arm intercepted by the brute who had helped carry the Font. Pulling back one meaty fist, the warthog-like leviathan hammered its hand into the charred one's chest, flattening the king's warrior.

Their struggle went ignored, the bodyguards' attention focused on their charge. They didn't know what to do as the metal between Crafter and doppelgänger dissolved, and Alec's flesh began to merge with The Scourge's back. Exhausted, Alec let his head slump forward, and his face fused to the back of the king's skull.

"NO!" The Scourge screamed one more time, taking a last futile step and stretching a hand out to beg for aid.

"No…" he cried pitifully as their bodies distorted. The two figures warped, twisting as they fused together.

The flash of light that followed was brilliant, and with it came a release of heat and a clap of thunder.

*　　*　　*

Someone was there, kneeling in armor that was carved with intricate designs, yet built for function. The armor pulsed as if alive. Looking up, the man surveyed his surroundings before he stood, brushing the dust from his armor and studying his taloned gauntlets.

"Sylvain," when he spoke, his voice was level and calm. "Release the Seer. She may be of use to us yet."

The charred one hesitated, the dagger he had plucked from the ground still raised to strike out at the brute and Veleda.

"Let's fulfill our end of the bargain. See to it that her family is released immediately." Dropping the knife, Sylvain bent to retrieve his sword, but found the king's foot pressing the blade to the floor.

"Alive."

Sylvain seemed about to protest, but the king clenched his fist, and the burned one's cleaver appeared in his hand, where it aged, rotted, and vanished in a plume of ash and dust. Understanding the threat, the soldier hurried to comply.

Pointing to two of his four guards, the king continued, "Go to New York and stop the assault on the glen." He turned his attention to the others, "You two, head to the library. There is no point in wasting resources anymore. No-one will refuse my new terms. After all, who can stop a Crafter?" the king chuckled. "And bring Commander Frederick here. I have a proposal for him."

The men did not hesitate to follow his command.

Satisfied, the king marched to his balcony, motioning to be followed. "Dream-walker!"

Hesitantly, Veleda looked around the room. When nobody moved, she realized the king had addressed her. It seemed that everyone had been watching and waiting for her response.

Waving everyone else away, the king stared over his lands, his hands resting on the balcony railing.

"You tried to kill me, Seer of Neviah." He continued to stare away into the distance; his voice calm and level. "But I understand why."

Loosening one gauntlet, the king exposed a hand. "I am offering you a full reprieve if you can carry out a very special mission for me. I don't wish to discuss the details aloud."

The king's face was impassive, impossible to read. Placing her palm on his, Veleda focused on his thoughts.

The darkness she remembered and feared—the brutality and sadism of The Scourge—was still there, but it was being kept at bay by the kindness, hope, and secret optimism she had felt in Alec. That part of him was grander now, fully in control, and holding back the darkness.

She saw him negotiating to return lands to the people; not the leaders of old who wished to remain in power, but denizens of the dreamscape who would work together to ensure the welfare of all.

She saw the Sandmen released and returning to duty.

She saw, too, what he wanted her to do. She saw the care home, she saw the burned and charred body of the man Alec loved, and saw herself guiding him into the dreamscape.

She broke away, smiling. With a deep bow, she said, "As my king commands."

Grinning in kind, Alec LeGuerrier shot her a wink only she could see. "Hurry," he said softly, "we have a kingdom to rule."

FIN

About the Author

Stephen Coghlan is an ever-expanding multi-genre, small-house published author who writes out of Canada's National Capital, who started writing in his teens for the same reason most young men do anything, to try and impress someone they have a crush on. The love of the written word outlasted that relationship, and while Stephen may have matured as a person and an author, his sense of humor has remained deceptively juvenile.

You can find out more on his website, http://www.scoghlan.com

More from Stephen Coghlan

Series

GENMOS: THE GENETICALLY MODIFIED SPECIES Trilogy
After disappearing from existence, Devlin Keper returns from his eight-year exile in order to gather his fifteen children, bio-engineered weapons known as Genmos, in an attempt to protect them from the government that first ordered them created, then wanted them destroyed.

Book 1: Gathering Storms (2017)
Book 2: Crossroads   (2020)
Book 3: Conclusions (Coming Soon)

THE NOBILIS SAGA:
If Nozomi had known that the discovery of the giant alien would lead to her parents' deaths, her brother being lost into a coma and merging with the alien called Nobilis, and a world dying in a fiery apocalypse caused by her hand, she would have just stayed in bed. Now she and her secretly-surviving-sibling struggle to stay one step ahead of all the fraughts of the cosmos in a rickety spaceship captained by a grizzled veteran-turned-janitor with just as many secrets as her, an alien princess and her enslaved husband, four children who may not be the same species, but are closer than siblings, and a scientist with the social graces of rotting meat.

Together, they must survive the storms that the galaxy throws against them, which includes greedy mega-corporations, raiders, pirates, the occasional band of slavers, and their own phantoms from the past.

Book 1: Seedling (2019)
Book 2: Loam/Radix (In Progress)

Novellas

50 SHADES OF NEIGH: (2020)
The Alternate-Edwardian-Period, Human/Centaur Crop-Opera Erotica you've never known you've wanted…

As The Great War begins, Clopia, Crowned Princess of the half-human/half-horse mercenary peoples known as Centaurs, must find a new means for her peoples or have them face the horror of the trenches.

A MOLLUSK AMONG MAN: (Coming Soon)
What would you do if you were nothing but a brain in a top-notch, ultra-modern artificial body that is everything that you are not on the inside?

How would you live if your every action could find you dragged back to jail, to be used as cheap labor, in a system designed to keep you permanently incarcerated?

Roca is forced to ask himself those questions and more as he finds himself recently paroled in a modern world where the economy is only held together by paranoia and the blood of the penal business. Forced to hide who he is in order to survive, Roca struggles to piece his life back together and carve a new future, while battling the demons that dragged his past self into a living hell.

More from Dark Brew Press

Bergden and Alyssa Crane are dutiful citizens of the Regime. Bergden, a Regime blackjack and Alyssa, a faithful wife, do what they can to provide for their son, James even when it means sacrificing their very freedom. But when Bergden is accused of treason, the Cranes must flee for their lives to escape the terrible reach of the Regime. During the escape, Bergden and Alyssa become separated.

Now, Bergden and Alyssa will do whatever they must, and against all odds, to unite their family. With the tyrannical Chancellor Kroft hunting them night and day, both must discover their inner strengths to conquer their fears and find each other's arms.

Little do they realize that a greater threat lurks in the shadows.

Love is commitment and never without cost...

Samir Amin has dedicated his life in service to the Nergal, an ancient organization that monitors and polices the inter-dimensional beings on our world and the magic that summons them. The only dark mark on his career is his close friendship with Anela Masterson—a being that was long ago trapped in a human body and forced to live near powerless in our world.

When Anela introduces him to Keeler Lim, another being trapped like her, on the condition he keeps it a secret from the Nergal, he does so reluctantly. Things only become more complicated when Anela is kidnapped by a madman who wants to release her darkness on the world and, unwilling to be forced to stand on the sidelines, Samir asks Keeler to help him find and rescue her.

It is a decision that causes Samir to be faced with a choice between love and duty—and it could cost him his life.